THE OBSI

A COLLECTION ~.

STEPH MINNS

Cover Artwork by Steph Minns

Copyright © 2016 Steph Minns
All rights reserved. No part of this publication may be reproduced without prior permission of the author.

ISBN-13:978-1541183353

ISBN-10:1541183355

Contents

1.......Bend In The Road
17.....A Shadow Of His Former Self
33.....Maricella
52.....New Town
72.....The Bus To Texcatl
91.....Carousel
113...I Thought You'd Gone Forever
131...The Halloween Party
150...Tiny Claws
173...The Sideways Dancing Woman
202...The Chrysalis
218...Bloody Christmas

Acknowledgements

Thanks to my fellow members of the Stokes Croft Writers group for their invaluable support.
Our writing group website is
www.stokescroftwriters.com

Bend in the Road

Steve didn't take this particular route to Dalford often, but he knew it well enough to realise he'd probably taken a wrong turn somewhere. Squinting at the upcoming road sign through the gathering darkness, he managed to read 'Dalford 6 miles,' pointing left, which reassured him he was still going in the right direction at least.

Humming, he turned up the heater of the old van. The country road verges slid by his peripheral vision, bone-stick hawthorns and sharp fingers of alder, poking over worn drystone walls, typical of this area of Somerset. Occasionally the warm glow of lights from farmhouse windows somewhere across the fields caught his eye, and he wished he were indoors now in a cosy room beside a roaring fire. It was getting bitterly cold. He wondered if maybe he should have taken the main road route, but that was the long way round, and Marie was waiting, probably with some wine already opened on the kitchen top. His hands-free buzzed cheerily, its cherry-pink alert button popping at him from the dash holder.

"I've got a lasagne in the oven, Steve. Will you be much longer?" His wife's voice was tense and he could read the irritation in it.

"Sorry Sal, the boss has just sent me on an emergency job, so don't wait for me. It's a burst pipe so I'll be pretty late, I expect."

He wasn't comfortable with the lie.

"Oh, I see."

He knew that stiff Sal tone, the one that would explode with anger later as she accused him of having an affair, of losing interest in her. It had always been the same accusation over the past year, but this time she'd got it right. There was no job but there was Marie. His marriage to Sal had become a dead-end road long ago, bitter, strained, but at last he'd had the balls to admit it to himself and this weekend he was determined to sit down with Sal and say 'lets call it a day.' It was the least he owed her, and himself, he reasoned. They could both make fresh starts, take a shot at trying to be happy again.

Lost in thought, he pulled up at the junction. Dalford 6 miles, said the sign, pointing left. Surely he'd just passed that sign only minutes ago? He felt he recognised a particularly gnarled, overgrown elder that grabbed at the passing cars just before the sign too. Turning left anyway, Steve started to gather speed and had just rounded a bend when he was confronted by a set of temporary traffic lights. Pulling up, he tapped a frustrated rhythm on the steering wheel. His van headlights picked out the red and white men-at-work sign so that it glowed eerily in the darkness on the verge. Softly falling snow started to patter at the windscreen, while the van engine hummed and the radio purred '80's pop classics. He waited for the light to turn to green.

On his way once more, his thoughts turned to Sal again. How long had they been married? Three years? It had fallen sour pretty quickly. One day he'd been sent on a job to a pasty shop in Wells, where he'd met shop assistant, Marie. They'd chatted, laughed, got along like old friends, and at the end of the day as he'd been packing up his tools, she'd smiled cheekily and handed him her phone number on a napkin. So Steve, who had never even considered being unfaithful before, had suggested they meet for a drink, just a drink, nothing more. But a beer and a pasty in a local pub later and Steve was sold. Marie, smelling deliciously of cinnamon and roses, took his mind away from the glooms of his marriage with her amusing tales of her life and cheerful banter.

Now here he was en route to Marie's home and Steve sweated with nervous anticipation that tonight might turn out to be a more than a 'just friends' moment. They were both attracted to each other, that was obvious, so where else could it eventually go?

Coming round the bend, he could see the blood-red reflection of the traffic lights on the wet road, and there was the men-at-work sign again, although there were no men at work at this time in the evening. How had he managed to drive in a loop and come back to this point again? He'd not turned off anywhere. The fact these lights were even here was odd, as there was no sign of any machinery parked nearby, waiting for daylight before the ripping up and crunching of tarmac began, and no cones or plastic barriers sat by the roadside either. So why the lights blocking his lane? There was no traffic coming towards him, and the road was empty.

"Typical of this bloody council," Steve muttered.

He was irritated now and began tapping a finger on the gearstick as he waited for green. Minutes passed as his exasperation grew. Marie would be waiting and the lights were not changing. He selected her number on his phone but there was no signal, only an odd low buzzing sound coming through the phone. Of course, he was in the middle of the countryside between towns, he reasoned.

Snow was gathering on the branches of a large oak tree in the field beside the road, and Steve watched as the crystals fell like feathers onto the dark road.

"Come on," he cursed the lights. "Turn green, for Godsake."

Bearing in mind the road had no other traffic he considered just driving around them, presuming they'd got a fault and were stuck on red. But something about doing that made him feel uneasy, as though someone, somewhere, would see him on a hidden traffic camera. So he waited and tried calling Marie again to explain he was running late. Again, all he could hear was the odd static buzz. Suddenly the signal connecting light came to life and he was sure he heard a phone ring tone, faint, as though buried somehow underground. A whispering voice broke through, but it was not Marie's.

"Choose. Red green red green. Go or stop?"

"Yes, you must choose. Go or wait."

"He has to choose!"

The hissing faint voices coming from the speaker appeared to be having a conversation among themselves.

"Hello, who is this?" Steve ventured.

Then the phone cut out again. He shuddered, baffled, staring at the windscreen wipers chasing away the gathering snow in front of him. Had he just picked up a signal from someone else's' mobile nearby? But he could see no house lights either side of the road, just the dark, snowy countryside. Odd too, he thought, that the whispers had talked about exactly what he'd been debating to himself.

"To hell with it."

Steve urged the van slowly forward and swept around the red light into the opposite lane, pulling back into the left again to continue up the road. As he did so he was sure he caught a glimpse in the rear view mirror of something large and dark alighting in the oak tree behind him, a tattered shadow. Snow fell from the branch it had landed on and scattered on the roadside. What sort of a bird was that, Steve wondered? Mindful the road was slippery, he drove carefully on until he reached the next junction. There was the 'Dalford 6 miles' sign again and this was definitely the junction he'd just come through.

"What the hell is going on?"

He was sure he'd made no turns, left or right. The signs must have been messed about by kids, he reasoned, and this time he made a deliberate right turn, the opposite direction to the sign pointing to Dalford.

Rounding a bend after a minute or two of driving, he came across the same temporary lights and the old oak beside the road again.

"No way."

Uneasiness stabbed him hard in the stomach. The light was at red. Steve automatically pulled up and tried calling Marie again. As he was about to select her number, the set crackled to life with the odd buzz once more, and a male voice barked at him.

"Don't go through the red. They'll get you if you go through the red again. They try to fool people, test them."

"Who? What are you talking about?"

Steve was angry now. What the hell was this? He became aware of movement up in the oak beside the road and of two, three, spindly dark shapes, like bloated black refuse sacks, landing in the branches. He was about to open the driver's door when the voice that had warned him about the red light croaked at him again.

"No. Don't go out there."

Unsure, instead he locked the door. A squabble of angry voices came over the line, and he was certain he could hear muttered threats.

"Shut up!"

"Don't tell him that, fool. You'll spoil the game."

"Yes, don't give it away."

The male voice had gone, and only the odd muttering and hissing remained.

"Who are you and what is this game?" Steve demanded, but his outburst was met with silence. The signal faded out again, the tiny light vanishing.

Unnerved, Steve leaned to peer up at the bird-things waiting in the tree. Their huddled black shapes were partly concealed by the branches and the darkness, but he sensed they were staring at him, watching, waiting for him to make a move. The light stayed on red. He swung the van into a three-point turn, wheels spinning in the snow in his haste. He decided that he wouldn't go through the red light again, just go back the way he'd come and take the next turnoff, whichever direction it said. As the van gathered speed, the black bird-like shapes took off from the tree and Steve was horrified to see they appeared more human than avian in his rear view mirror. Long skeletal legs hung down below their sack-like bodies, while their wings flapped slowly, wings that he guessed must have at least a six foot span. The faces, as they gained on him, had the appearance of burnt, blackened human skulls on swan-like necks, and he could make out glowing red eyes.

Panicking, Steve put his foot down, all fear of an oncoming car as he slewed across the slippery road gone in his terror. The first of the creatures caught up and he heard a scrabble on the roof and the van dip as the thing landed on it.

"Fuck!"

He swung the van sharply to the left and whatever it was went skittering off to flap into the hedge, screeching with an unearthly wail. The others had nearly closed the distance now and Steve prayed for a turning to appear, leading anywhere, just off this road. All he could do was carry on forwards, wrestling the van as it slid and bounced across the country road. Even a house, he decided, where he could pull into a drive and beg shelter would be welcome, but there were no cosy windows aglow anywhere now in this desolate countryside, only the seemingly endless road.

At last, his headlights picked up a road sign and he slowed to take the junction. Dalford 6 miles, the sign now pointing both ways to the left and right.

"No!"

He swung the van right, managing to keep it on the road. He dreaded what would happen if he crashed and found himself stranded out here, with those things. Glancing in the rear view mirror, he could see the dark, bulbous shapes with their skinny legs and glowing eyes, gliding on silent wings across the junction, although they appeared to be holding back a little now.

Desperate, Steve shouted aloud as he rounded a bend and there, like an ominous red eye staring him down, were the temporary lights again in the distance. The dash phone crackled into life as he automatically started to slow down, remembering the warning from the mystery voice earlier.

"Red green, choose, choose," the hissing inhuman voices mocked.

"What will he do? Stop or go?"

The voice that had originally warned him not to run the light suddenly broke in urgently.

"Take the next left before the lights."

"There is no turn off," Steve yelled. "No fucking turnings before those lights."

"There will be. I will make one," the voice reassured him.

Just before he reached the lights a mysterious lane appeared to the left, emerging as though from a heat haze. Steve didn't question, just slid the van around into it, and floored the accelerator. Now he was terrified that he may have just minutes to get clear of the area before the lane vanished again.

He was aware of the hissing voices shrieking in disapproval.

"No!"

"He can't do that....not fair."

"Curse you for helping him."

The voices were fainter though, breaking up as though interference was blocking the signal and cutting them off.

"Thank you. Thank you, whoever you are." Steve muttered aloud to his saviour voice.

The bird-skeleton monsters were not following, had vanished, and the lane suddenly ended at a T-junction. Steve's gut twisted in anticipation as he pulled up, his headlights picking up the road sign.

This time no Dalford, just left to Wells 2 miles and right to Bristol 10 miles. Steve broke out in a sweat, wondering if this was another trick and if he should do anything for a moment. Head spinning with the dilemma, he sat in the van, hands shaking on the wheel as the snow kissed the van's hot bonnet, melting away. His was the only vehicle on the road in the darkness. Taking a deep breath, he made his decision and headed right for Bristol city.

After a few moments, car headlights appeared a way off in front of him. Another vehicle, or was this another visual trick to lull him into a sense of false security? But it was a car, a real car with a woman at the wheel, and her headlights chased the shadows around his cab as their vehicles passed. Then she was gone again, tail lights vanishing up the road. Red lights, like that cursed traffic light and the eyes of those things, Steve thought and shuddered. He passed though a village where TVs flickered through curtains, and normal, real people lived their daily lives. He'd never been more relieved to see a petrol station in his life as he pulled onto the forecourt of a local Texoco's. Turning off the engine, he sat in bewilderment for a while, trying to make sense of what had just happened.

Had he passed through some portal into a parallel dimension or something? And who had his saviour been? Gathering himself together and forcing himself to stay calm, he made his way unsteadily into the filling station shop and approached the assistant.

"Can you tell me if there are any roadworks due to start around here soon?"

"Not that I know of, mate," the young man shrugged. "Any petrol?"

No, no thanks, just this."

He shoved the cold can of lemonade forward, aware his throat was as dry as old parchment. Back in the van he barely tasted the drink. This time when the phone rang it was definitely Marie that answered.

"Marie, something weird happened...I'm sorry... I'm not even sure where I am. Somewhere between Wells and Bristol. I...got lost."

"Are you OK, Steve? You sound a bit shaky."

"Yeah, yeah I'll be with you soon."

Realising he really needed directions, he went back into the shop to ask the assistant the way to Dalford.

"Yeah, turn left out of here an' next junction right. You can't miss the sign."

"Thanks."

Maybe he should just ring Marie and cancel. The thought of leaving this main road to travel back onto those unmarked, winding country roads again frankly alarmed him. To just carry on into Bristol with its busy, well lit streets and home would make more sense. But he couldn't let Marie down and he badly needed to talk to someone familiar and comforting right now. So Steve drove to the junction and turned right. The sign for right said 'Dalford 1mile,' and left was to some village he'd vaguely heard of. After five minutes he found himself at another junction and he groaned in disbelief as he read the sign 'Dalford 6 miles.'

"No way!"

He performed another three-point turn and followed the route he'd just come, remembering the filling station assistant's directions. He expected to find himself safely back on the main road therefore, with its streetlights, the petrol station and cluster of houses. But instead he found himself turning a bend where a green traffic light lit up a huge, gnarled oak ahead of him.

Stomach clenched, he drove faster. Maybe if he could make it through the green light he'd be free, the voices and the bird-horrors wouldn't come. But the light changed mockingly to red, just as he was getting close to it, and he had no choice but to overshoot it in the snow. Braking a little way past the unit, he looked back to check the tree, nervous sweat breaking out down his back. No bird-things were there and Steve expelled a relieved breath.

As he started to pull away again there was a thump on the roof and the van rocked slightly as something landed on it. Steve braked hard. Claws scraped along the roof as something heavy slid across it, and then a grinning skull face on a long black feathered neck appeared, peering in at him through the windscreen.

Steve screamed and watched, frozen, as more black shapes dived out of the snow-filled air to land on the road and start hopping towards the van. He counted five, lumbering closer, dragging their bat-wings along the ground, heads bobbing and weaving side to side on their swannish necks. Steve started to sob and the snow fell thicker, covering his tyre tracks so, soon, no one would even know he had ever passed this way.

Desperately punching 999 into his phone was the only thing he could think to do, however futile it may be, but the only sound he could hear was the crackling tone again and the muttering voices, talking distractedly among themselves.

"Didn't learn, did he?"

"No. Had a chance. Blew it."

"Yep. Blew it."

"Some humans just never learn."

A Shadow of His Former Self

Everyone said Doug was colourless, anonymous. Pleasant and kindly, folk agreed, but nondescript all the same. A forty-plus unemployed bachelor, Doug was pretty much invisible, even to his own family sometimes, although he'd always call round to his elderly mum's on his way back from the supermarket at the edge of Bream council estate. Doug lived in a tatty one bed flat on the estate, and the 80's geometric print curtains at his windows were faded and dusty. Sometimes he looked at them and thought they sort of summed up his existence, outdated and worn out, but he couldn't really afford to buy new ones. His benefits didn't stretch to such frivolous things as curtains, even second-hand ones.

His mum always greeted him the same way when he dropped by.

"'Allo love, been up to anything nice lately?"

Doug would shrug, pick uneasily at the bobbles on his shapeless jumper (one of many) and reply.

"Nah, just the usual stuff."

But today Doug seemed more animated as he sat down at the kitchen table for his usual cup of tea with his mum.

"I had a chat with Bel this morning in the lift." His face lit up at the memory.

"Bel?"

His mum turned from the fridge, all ears.

"Yeah. She lives in the flat below with her girls. Bel's nice, really kind. We chat when we bump into each other in Tesco's. She's divorced and her dad's from Jamaica. Her eldest girl, Aisha, is brill at 'Viking War.' She gave me some good tips for getting onto level 9."

"That's nice, dear." His mum smiled encouragingly. "Will you invite her in for tea sometime?"

The animation faded from Doug's face as though a balloon had suddenly popped behind it. He shrugged, gazing uncomfortably at the Formica table top.

"Probably not. She might think I'm sort of...well, trying to chat her up and be creepy."

"No, Doug. It's just a nice, neighbourly thing to do," his mum responded. "You need to get out more, meet new people. You fester in that flat all day, and you've no hobbies. You need a hobby."

"I tried volunteering at the charity shop, didn't I? Then they asked me to leave when I kept messing up the till."

Doug's resigned expression closed down the conversation, and his mum sighed and rose to busy herself at the sink. He could feel her daggers of disapproval but he really had tried, tried to get a job, make new friends. When he'd made friends with the boys down the end of the corridor last summer someone had gossiped, started trouble. The older kids had started calling him a 'paedo' and he'd had to endure cold glares from people on the estate who'd known him for years, people who should have known better. Someone had even shoveled dog mess through his letterbox on one occasion.

As Doug made his lonely way back to his flat, he pondered how maybe it would be nice to ask Bel in for a cuppa perhaps when he next bumped into her. But at the back of his mind, he suspected that he'd do no such thing and life would continue to slide past in its usual grey, dreary routine. That prospect was depressing, but so was the realization that he'd need to confront himself head-on if he was ever to make something of his life. It was easier to just leave things as they were, Doug decided, safety in the familiar. Anyway, he was too old to change his ways now, wasn't he?

***

It was Friday, pub night. Doug, in baggy jeans and one of his better jumpers, sauntered across the estate towards the squat 1960's red brick carbunkle that was his favourite watering hole. The late summer sun hadn't quite set and it cast his shadow before him. The shadow bore a resemblance to a troll lurching along the pavement, its head a blurry outline due to his frizzy mop of ginger hair.

"Hey, Mr Blobby!"

A kid shouted out as he passed the playground.

Doug barely flinched, being used to such abuse by the local tearaways. He'd been the target for abuse and bullying since his schooldays after all, so it no longer really touched him.

"No bloody respect for their elders anymore," he mumbled to himself, but privately he had to admit the Mr. Blobby reference could perhaps fit, looking at his shadow as it plodded along with him. Doug had never really studied his shadow before, and he smiled, seeing the comical side to the insult now.

At last he reached the refuge of the pub and was swamped by the usual chatter and roars of laughter as he stepped through the door, his feet sticking to the worn carpet, stained with years of dried-in booze. His regular booze-buddies were there, baldy man Reg, Bob the scaffolder and his brother, Ant. Doug gave them a quick wave as he made his way to the bar to get the usual round in. They all drank the same local ale, so no problem asking what they wanted. No one ever thought of trying something else. Why would they? 'Belly Buster' pale ale was a local brew and they were proud of it. God knows there was little else to be proud about in this down-trodden Northern town with its dirty canals and abandoned factories.

It was dark by the time Doug left the pub at closing, so no sun cast his shadow now. But as he passed under the overspill from the floodlights of the empty football stadium, he fancied his faint shadow, thrown ahead of him by their vivid glare, had changed somehow. It looked leaner, taller, and it seemed to stride forcefully along, joined to his shambling feet.

"Mr Blobby indeed."

Doug chuckled to himself, belching a beery one and deciding it must be a trick of the light. Then he thought no more of it.

***

But over the next few days Doug noticed his shadow was definitely changing as he shuffled about his usual business, and it definitely wasn't the effect of beer or his imagination. It had grown taller, slimmer, the head nothing like his fuzzy mop-head. The shadow had what looked like a shaved scalp and the outline of ears protruding. He stopped one sunny morning on the way to the corner shop to stare at the shadow he cast on a factory wall, turning his head and swiveling his gaze quickly to the side to try and catch its profile. It definitely had a sharp beaky nose, quite unlike his own, and he frowned, puzzled, before striding quickly on. The shadow paced alongside him, slipping along the wall, sliding over objects he passed, the pillar-box on the corner of Dean Street and the peeling doors of a garage. When he reached the newsagent's, he stopped in front of the window to study his reflection, trying to see how his frizzy head could suddenly become a beaky skull, but his grimacing mirror-image looked normal enough in the glass, just his usual, familiar self.

'I must be losing my mind,' Doug thought desperately. 'This can't be real. It must be a hallucination.'

But the shadow was undeniably morphing into something very unlike himself. He eyed it nervously each time he left the flat after that, studying it to see what new feature it had developed. After the nose and ears it grew long skinny hands that hung like claws beside it. When he swung his arms the shadow would obligingly swing its arms too, but those menacing hands didn't look like they were cast by Doug's podgy digits.

Then he stopped going out to the shops during the day, only leaving the flat after sunset but before the street lights came on, so he no longer had to see the changing shadow. When his mum phoned to see why he'd not been over for a while, he made a lame excuse about feeling poorly. He couldn't bear to admit he was scared of his own shadow.

"Make sure you go to the doctor's if you're not feeling good," his mum insisted.

Doug debated that maybe he should go, tell the doctor what was happening. Maybe they'd give him some pills to help, send him to counseling or something. But that thought terrified him as much as the shadow, so he stayed put in the flat. During the day he'd sit in with the curtains drawn, and in the evening he'd leave all the main lights and every lamp in the flat blazing so that the rooms were filled with light, and his bulky form cast no shadow anywhere. But he knew it was still there, although it was invisible, just waiting for a chance to make itself known again. A deep feeling of dread began to seep into Doug, and he noticed other changes starting to creep in too.

His vision was growing dimmer. At times he'd see a sort of shimmering strobe effect in front of his eyes and then everything would become darker, as though he were looking through a smoky glass filter. After a while it seemed to resolve itself and everything he looked at would be normal, flooded with colour once again. The green flowers on the carpet would be green once more and the kitchen tiles would revert back to their cheerful lemon. Alarmed, Doug made an appointment at the opticians', but his gut feeling told him that this was not a problem with his eyesight but had something to do with the shadow. He didn't know how he knew this, but the thought terrified him. The shadow was changing him somehow, intruding into his very being.

***

Outside, the day was a drizzling grey. Autumn was drawing in again and for Doug that was a relief. There would be no bright sunlight to cast any shadows today. He walked for over an hour, trying to resolve the dilemma in his mind. He needed to show this phenomena to someone else, and if someone else could see it too he'd know for sure he wasn't losing his mind. Mum had left yesterday for a budget break in Minorca with Aunt May so he couldn't ask her. Maybe he should call one of his drinking buddies, but he reckoned they'd just laugh at him. While being the centre of a joke and ribbing was not new to Doug, he knew this was serious and not a subject for jesting at his expense.

In desperation, he suddenly thought of Bel. She would help. She'd always been nice to him and he trusted she wouldn't laugh if he asked her to check his shadow and describe what she saw. He'd tell her, show her, ask her to put a lamp behind him so he cast a shadow on the wall. Then they would both see that horrible shape that wasn't him, and it would confirm he wasn't going mad and it wasn't all in his imagination.

Doug returned home through the grey streets as the sky began to drizzle with rain. Knocking uneasily on Bel's door, he started to wonder if this was such a good idea. The girls would be at school so this wouldn't scare them, but maybe Bel would think he was bonkers. She didn't really know him, only for a passing chat, if he were honest. Suddenly desperately lonely, Doug was about to turn for the lift to go back to his own flat, when Bel answered the door. Her face broke into a surprised smile, as though he were the last person she'd expected to see there.

"Oh, hello Doug. Is everything OK?"

"Um. I hope you don't mind, but could I ask you to check something for me please?"

"Sure, come in."

His neighbour stepped aside to let him into the hall. He followed her to the living room where she turned off the reggae music she'd been playing. Her dreadlocks were wound up into a scarf and she was wearing old joggers, so he guessed she'd been in the middle of housework.

"What can I do for you, Doug?"

Doug fumbled nervously for words, knowing how stupid and weird this would sound, aware that he probably looked slightly alarming with his disheveled hair and unshaven face.

"My shadow doesn't look like me anymore. Would you mind shining a lamp on me so I can show you what I mean? It will need to be a bright one so we get a good, clear outline."

Bel's eyes became wary and her mouth tightened into a thin line, the welcoming smile gone. But she obliged all the same, although Doug noted she kept a good distance between them. They both looked at his shadow, flung across the living room wall. Rigid with anticipation, his stomach clenching, Doug turned one way, then another, studying his outline. It looked normal, like him with his mop-head and pudgy hands, a recognizable Mr Blobby.

"Looks fine to me, Doug. What did you expect to see?" Bel was looking at him uneasily, clutching the ceramic lamp from her sideboard as though she thought it could make a good self-defence weapon now if needed.

"I...I thought...sorry Bel. Thanks."

He fled for the door, embarrassed and relieved at the same time. His shadow was back as it should be. But as he fumbled his key in his front door, hand shaking, it suddenly occurred to him that the shadow was playing games, trying to fool him, and it was hiding from other people's sight.

***

Waking and turning over in bed the following morning, Doug saw the shadow sitting in the chair in the corner of the bedroom, staring at him. At least, he felt it was staring at him, although it had no face as such, just the outline of a bald head and that frightening beaky profile when it turned sideways on.

"Please God," he whimpered. "Make it go away, make it leave me alone."

As though it understood, the shadow stood up and left the room, gliding along the wall and out into the hallway. Now an independent, almost solid black shape, it seemed to need no light source in order to exist. It didn't need Doug either, he realized with horror. It had taken on a life of its own.

Finally gathering courage, Doug followed it out into the hall, where he found it crouching by the front door like a panther about to spring at its next meal. Letting out a little scream, Doug bolted for the kitchen, slamming the door behind him. Shaking and close to tears, he waited a while, forcing himself to calm down.

It's not happening, it's a hallucination, he told himself. When he finally steeled his nerves to open the door a little way to peer out, the shadow had gone. He shambled nervously from room to room, looking for it, dreading to find it but needing to know where it was, at the same time. As he entered the living room he spotted the tall, dark shape sitting in his favourite chair, watching him silently.

"What the hell are you?" Doug stammered.

The dark man rose from the chair and slid towards him along the wall. Doug's legs gave way and he slumped to the carpet, dizzy, his vision swimming into that bizarre dark filter again. The shadow watched for several minutes, hands on hips as though it were deep in thought, as Doug tried to struggle to his feet. Doug cried out in panic. He could barely see the surrounding room now as his vision grew darker. What he could see was a shimmering doorway against the magnolia-painted wall, and he was sure he could make out more of the shadow men beyond it, moving slowly around, peering out into the room. He managed to stagger to the armchair, gasping, and the shadow figure retreated to the far side of the room where it merged with the gloom beyond the floor lamp. Doug lay exhausted and weeping in his chair, thinking it would be fine if someone could help, if only he could reach the phone.

To call who? His heart was thumping like a metronome in his chest, marking his last minutes on Earth, it seemed to him. Tick tock. He could feel the shady intruder draining his energy like a leech sucking blood.

"Let me go. Leave me alone, please."

His voice was barely a whisper and the shadow stood in the corner, studying him as the panther watches, calculating its moment to strike the prey. Tears of desperation and fear rolled down Doug's face, and he thought 'so it ends like this. They'll assume I had a stroke or heart attack.'

The shadow stepped softly forward until its own feet joined up to Doug's bare, chubby feet again. The last thing he was aware of was a slippery, silver voice which said simply.

"I know you."

***

Three weeks after the odd visit from her upstairs neighbour, Bel noticed a foul liquid dripping through her bathroom ceiling. Assuming at first it was a burst waste pipe, she sprayed air freshener around and called the council. Then she decided she'd better alert Doug in case he was unaware of the leak. She was a little wary of him since that odd thing about his shadow, but she honestly couldn't believe there was any harm in him. He'd seemed such a pleasant, inoffensive man, just a little slow and confused.

The flies swarming the inside of the windows in Doug's flat alerted her that something was wrong, even before she'd rung the doorbell. When the police arrived twenty minutes later, they broke down the door and ushered the gathering neighbours away, but not before the stench of putrefying flesh had permeated the whole landing, sending them gagging. Bel watched from her kitchen as the ambulance crew wheeled the body bag across the car park, wishing she'd given Doug more time that last day he'd called with his odd request. Another invisible man, living alone and dying alone in a council sink estate.

Nobody saw the shadow watching from the stairwell, a blacker than black shape that seemed to take on the form of a tall, gangly man. After the ambulance had left, it slid across the wall and slipped back into Doug's empty flat through the letterbox. Inside, it folded silently into Doug's favourite chair, and listened contentedly as Doug's soul screamed and fought to get out of its head. Maybe it smiled with shadow-lips as it savored its latest meal.

Maricella

Vienna 1838
2 February
Dear J.

You'll have no doubt heard the good news about my examination results by now, so I won't go into it again. I'm so excited at the prospect of returning home to you all next month, or should I say, relieved, after the events of the past weeks. Although I love Vienna in winter, with its glorious sparkling palaces and wonderful frosted parks, I have come to regard it now as a slightly dark place. I have the ticket for my passage home in front of me on my desk, as I write, and long to see those fields and hedgerows of Somerset again, and of course yourself and our dear Mama. How is she these days? I hope your chest is better, despite the damp weather. I will bring back some ointment, devised by an apothecary I have trained under, which many here swear by and may bring you some relief.

I feel I must tell you about something that has happened, a very sorry tale. I've just warmed some coffee and brandy, for it's bitter outside. I can scarce see the spires of St. Stephen's for the falling snow. I will try and make some sensible account of what took place and that makes me so glad at the prospect of leaving this city.

You've heard me speak of my friend, Harry Spencefield, in previous letters. Well, I'll start at the beginning so you can understand how things here developed. A month ago, Harry and I decided to stroll over to a district known as Hertzieg, a little off the beaten track but on the southern bank of the River Wien. We'd not explored this area at all, and it has a reputation for being slightly seedy, which drew us both, as you can imagine.

Crossing a wrought iron bridge, we found we'd left the wealthy properties with their pretty balconies and fairy-tale turreted rooms, behind. The streets here were narrow, lined with older buildings with something of the peeling gothic about them, and the gaslights were few and far between, adding an air of atmospheric gloom. I hope you can picture the scene. Harry was getting impatient to find the bordellos and drinking dens seething with absinthe-sodden artists we'd heard about, and we were just about to give up our quest and return the way we'd come, when we heard music drifting from an alleyway. Following it, we found the alley opened into a lively cobbled square, lined with bars and food stalls. We noticed many people filing into a small black-timbered building opposite, which bore a sign announcing 'Leipchek's Amazing Marionette Show.' Curious, we decided to go inside and catch the show.

We were ushered into a musty, lamp-lit cellar, where rows of wooden benches had been arranged in front of a make-shift stage. On the stage was a puppet booth, hung with grubby draperies and Harry laughed, saying he expected we'd be treated to an hour of torture now, entertained by puppets made from straw sack and button eyes.

But nothing could have been further from the truth. When the curtain fell back it revealed two of the most magnificent marionettes I have ever set eyes on. I can't profess to be any authority on these things, but they were obviously made with exquisite craftmanship. The female character had a painted face that looked quite real, and was dressed in blue silk and lace. The male soldier character was likewise very realistic and wore a detailed uniform. Both stood about three feet high and the puppeteers manipulated them with such skill they came uncannily alive under their guidance. The audience was spellbound, especially Harry, who seemed transfixed, and when the hat came round after the performance (the tale was a rather sad one about lost love) he gushed that he just had to meet the puppeteers and congratulate them.

Well we did, and they were rather ordinary, a red-haired man and two lads, who were his assistants. Harry enthused about how much he was taken by the marionettes, especially the lead female character, called Maricella. When he offered to buy it I saw a sly expression cross the man's face, and half-expected him to ask some ridiculous amount as he obviously realised Harry was smitten. But, to my surprise, he said he couldn't possibly sell her, nor any of the others, as they were his living and as dear to him as his children - the two grubby boys, I gathered.

Harry couldn't stop talking about the Maricella puppet all the way home, how beautiful she was, how her eyes were so blue and real-looking, that her hair was real human hair, not just painted onto her head. I was amused at first, and let him ramble on, but by the time we reached my lodgings he'd become quite obsessive about the thing. 'I must go back tomorrow night to see her again,' he insisted, and he seemed in a dream when we parted.

Over the next two weeks, Harry was noticeable by his absence. Previously, he'd call on me around seven o'clock of an evening, maybe with one or two of our fellow students in tow, and we'd all find a bar that served decent, cheap food. But he suddenly stopped doing this and, more worryingly, didn't turn up for lectures either, which concerned me as we were due to sit our final paper. No one else in our circle appeared to have seen him either when I asked around.

On the evening before we were to sit our last exam, I ran into him quite by chance as I left my lodgings to buy supper at the delicatessen on the corner. I'd intended staying in for some last minute study and not visit any bar, but to see the state of Harry shocked me, and I insisted on buying him a brandy.

He'd grown thin, his face full of stubble, and there was an oddness in his manner that alarmed me. He refused my offer of food, but gulped the brandy and gazed at me with such an odd expression I feared for his mental balance. 'She is so wonderful, I can barely bring myself to leave her for one minute,' he said.

'She is everything I ever wanted in a companion.' Who, I asked, assuming he had become smitten by some young woman he'd met, maybe even one of the ladies of the bordellos I was aware he frequented at times. 'Maricella, of course,' he replied with that glazed look. 'I have her, she is mine now.'

When I prodded further I realised he meant the marionette from the puppet show, and when he admitted that he hadn't bought it but stolen it after the make-shift theatre had closed one night, I was outraged. Those puppets are the man's livelihood to feed his family, I scolded him. How could you be so selfish and foolish? He became defensive then, insisting she had to be with him. 'She told me so in a dream,' he explained. 'She told me I had to rescue her from him, from Leipchek.' Baffled, I said no more, just called after him not to forget the examination in the morning as he fled for the door, but he didn't show up the next day. Nor did we see him again.

His body was pulled from the Danube two days ago. We were all shocked, of course. It was presumed by the authorities that Harry had slipped and fallen into the river to drown. They did not suspect foul play as there were no marks of a battering on his body, and it didn't appear he'd been robbed. It had crossed my mind that he'd leapt to his death in the freezing water, given the confused state I'd last seen him in.

Such a sorry end. Harry was popular for his good nature and humour. I, for one, will certainly miss him.

Love to all

Alex

10 February

Dear J.

I hope you and Mama are well.

This week I was given the grim task from our Head of Studies of clearing out Harry's lodgings and returning his personal belongings to his parents. He hadn't spoken about them much, although I knew they lived in Whitby. The Head gave me their address and money to cover. He'd already written to them with the terrible news.

Harry's landlord let me into his room, and as soon as I entered I felt uneasy. There was a faint perfume in the air, roses I believe, and there, bolt upright in the bed, was the Maricella puppet. He'd cut away its strings, which gave it even more of a life-like appearance, and it looked thoroughly unnerving as it sat there, a painted doll that could have been mistaken for a small child at first glance. I busied myself checking through drawers and cupboards in the bare attic room, feeling like a peeping tom. Harry's life sadly packed into the travelling trunk I found under the bed, I turned my attention to the doll.

While I worked, I'd had an odd feeling that someone was watching me. I wondered if Harry's ghost was in the room but then chided myself for the fancy. I was a man of science and dealt with facts, not the irrational. But all the same, when I turned to look at the Maricella puppet, I could have sworn the head had rotated on the wooden neck, and its huge blue eyes were actually looking at me with disapproval. No it was just the way the eyes were painted, I told myself, varnished to catch the light and appear to move in their sockets. Or maybe there was some special mechanism inside that operated somehow without a human hand to manipulate it, maybe by gravity on the tilt of the head.

I picked it up with slight distain, noting that Harry (it could only have been he) had dressed it in a child-sized nightgown and had brushed out the blond hair as though ready for bed. I didn't dwell on what else he may have done to the puppet, but simply stuffed it into a spare sack I'd brought, intending to return it to the owner.

That evening I took it back to the theatre, ready to apologise for my poor friend's misdemeanour, and explain his odd state of mind. But the show had closed and gone. The owner of the building, who ran the bar above the cellar room, told me that Mr. Leipchek had taken his Amazing Marionette Show to Melk, a day away, so I stopped by the train station and paid the stationmaster to send it on. I had no idea where the puppet show would be, but I addressed it clearly to the Leipchek Marionette Show and hoped it would eventually get back to its rightful owner. As I handed the bundle over the counter, an odd thing happened. I felt a sharp stab in my wrist and, looking down, I saw some red marks appearing. I left the station and returned home, thinking to put some ointment on what I assumed was an insect bite on my wrist, but I was baffled to see what appeared to be a human bite-mark, as though small, child-sized teeth had sunken into my flesh. I didn't know what to make of it but the marks faded within the hour. The excitement of finding I had passed my exam the following morning swept away any more thought on it. We fellows went for a celebratory beer and got to talking of the one classmate missing from the table, Harry.

Tell Mama I have found some exquisite lace, as she requested, and will bring her some home, enough for a few dress collars at least.

All my best wishes

Alex

16 February

Dear J.

Things have been odd here since Harry's death. Most of my fellows have left already for their various home towns. All except Hans, of course, who is a native to Vienna.

Harry's landlord turned up at the college two days ago, asking for me. He handed over a journal that my friend had been keeping, explaining he'd found it in a drawer in the corner table, which I must have missed during my clear-out of his belongings. I brought it home, intending to post it on to his parents, but decided to sneak a look inside first. I suppose at the back of my mind I hoped it would give me some clue as to why Harry had lost his mind, and perhaps if he had planned suicide after all.

The contents were certainly alarming.

The journal started off normally, accounts of trips he'd made, thoughts on lectures and ideas to follow up on medical sources. Then it came to mentioning the Leipchek Marionette Show, and from then on it rambled about the Maricella puppet in the same obsessive, deluded way he'd done the last time I'd seen him and bought him a drink, talking as though she were a real, live woman he was having some sort of affair with.

The entries were mostly about 'conversations' he'd had with the puppet, and it seemed he believed the puppet was possessed by the spirit of a woman, called Maricella, who had been murdered by Leipchek himself. One entry runs (I have it before me) 'Maricella explained Leipchek had performed some sort of sorcery to bind her spirit to the wooden puppet he'd crafted. That's why she had so desperately reached out to me that night she'd seen me in the audience, to beg me to help her escape.'

It goes on in that manner, and is deeply disturbing. I don't believe any ghost is attached to the doll, of course, but it is upsetting to think he did and it all ended in his death. Having read these entries now I firmly believe poor Harry killed himself due to madness.

I intend sending the journal on to his parents in England, although I am a little reluctant to do so. Perhaps it would be kinder to let them carry on thinking he met with an accident, although I don't know how much the Head of Studies said in his letter, of course.

What a sorry episode it all is.

Anyway, I'll write more in the next few days, as it's getting late now.

Hearty greetings to you all. Kiss Mama for me.

Yours

Alex

26 February

Dear J.

It's snowing again and I'm struggling to stay warm in my attic rooms. Hans kindly invited me to his parent's home for luncheon yesterday. Being with such a lovely family raised my spirits. His grandmother speaks only German but we somehow communicated well enough. She plays the piano beautifully.

You'll not believe this. I felt prompted to look into the Leipchek marionettes, mainly as a diversion now studies have finished, so I took myself down to the bar where the puppet show had performed, hoping the owner could maybe tell me more. There I got into drinking with him. He's a most cheerful and genial fellow.

He revealed that both Leipchek and his father before him, who'd made most of the puppets, had something of a sinister reputation for meddling in the dark arts. He told me the father (now dead) had been an evil devil, and had boasted once in the bar that some of his puppets really did have souls, the spirits of people he'd killed and later fashioned a puppet likeness for. Of course no-one had believed that at the time, thinking him a rambling old drunk.

The same story was detailed in Harry's journal that I told you of, remember? Harry wrote about the supposed spirit of a young woman, trapped in the Maricella puppet, claiming Leipchek Jnr. had killed her. I presume Harry had heard the same stories about the Leipcheks, of course, when he'd re-visited the bar before stealing the puppet. Then he'd got it muddled in his head, convinced the puppet was telling him these things.

Poor Harry. His body was sent back on a ship to his parents for burial. God knows how terrible this all is for them.

I myself dreamed a few nights ago of a pretty, young, blonde woman with huge, cornflower blue eyes. I know you're rolling your eyes and chuckling now, but the dream was really intense and I can remember it in detail, even now. She clasped my hands desperately in the dream, imploring me to free her and demanding why had I sent her back to him? Of course I thought of the puppet and Harry, so put it down to recent events playing on my mind.

I had to pause in my writing just now. There was a most peculiar shrieking outside in the gardens. It's dusk here but light enough to still see the lawns and shrubs that run up the path to the street. I couldn't see anyone outside, but suppose it was an owl or some such, although I've not heard its' like before.

You mentioned in your last letter that your lungs are much improved lately. That's good news and I hope it continues.

Your brother

Alex

2 March
Dear J.

Some evenings I feel an unseen horror stalks on my tail and I hasten my steps to reach my lodgings after visiting the library or market. I beg you not to dismiss me as going addled in the brain. But I feel I need to unburden myself to someone who knows me well, and will not judge me harshly.

I have to tell you about this rather alarming episode. Just yesterday, I was cutting down the alleyway from the library when I saw a cowled shadow sliding along the wall, following me. When I stopped, it stopped. When I turned sharply, expecting to be coshed by a street robber, the alley was empty and there was no-one behind me. It clearly wore a brimmed hat, such as peasants and workmen wear in Vienna, and had long, straggly hair. I freely admit I broke into a run, all the way to the other end of the alley where it meets the main street, tumbling down the steps to the cobbles. Once among the bustle and noise of the citizens again, I felt a lot safer. I will avoid all alleyways and anywhere devoid of people from now on.

What was I doing at the library, I hear you ask? Well, I was curious to see if a Maricella had ever existed and had been reported missing or murdered. Would you believe, I found a newspaper article in the archives, detailing the disappearance of a seventeen year old heiress only two years ago. She'd vanished from a society ball, never to be seen again, and her name was Maricella Hofflan. I asked the librarian about this and she remembered the incident well as it had caused such an uproar at the time. She said that Leipchek Jnr. Had been arrested at one point as he'd been overheard threating the girl's father, who had publicly condemned his puppet show as 'unwholesome'. There was no evidence of foul play, however, and the authorities had been forced to release him. The photograph of the missing girl bore an uncanny likeness to the Maricella puppet that Harry had taken.

What an odd coincidence. How had Harry come by the information, I wonder?

It is snowing now and the hot chestnut vendor is out in the street. The glow from his barrel of coals is a cheery sight, shining through the railings, when most else is just grey and dark.

Looking forward to seeing you all in a few days.

Alex

6 March

Dear J.

You probably weren't expecting to hear from me so soon after the last letter, but I had to write again to let you know the schedule for my boat has changed and I probably won't reach Bristol until after midday on the Sunday now. If I catch the afternoon coach to Exeter I can be home by late evening.

An odd thing has started waking me at night lately, the sound of tip tapping feet outside in the corridor, like hob nail boots walking. When I first got up to investigate, ready to confront a robber, there was no one there. Each time I've jumped up to check and the corridor has been empty. As the landlord lives on the floor below, I'm sure I would have heard the footsteps go back down the stairs if it were he. He rarely bothers me anyway, only on rent day. The footsteps are certainly puzzling. Maybe ghosts do exist after all.

I had to break off writing just now to check the corridor. The footsteps were there again, and three nights ago I was sure I saw a pale woman crossing the lawn below my window, but she walked oddly, stiffly, not as a person walks. She wore a flimsy blue silk gown, despite there being a deep frost outside, which had not melted all day. She stared up at my window before walking off among the trees. I just have a feeling of dread now, of something building up. I certainly did not imagine the steps outside the door again.

I'll finish this letter another day as I need to venture out for some food now. I hope you and Mama are keeping warm and well.

***

Last night was terrifying. The steps in the corridor were louder and lasted longer, pacing up and down before stopping at my door. This time I dared not open the door to look. I saw the woman in blue flit across the frozen lawn around two in the morning as well, being up and unable to settle. She vanished before reaching the path and when I say vanished I mean she really did, right in front of my eyes, just fading away. I was left shaking afterwards. I wonder now if this is what poor Harry was experiencing, and which led him to despair so as to throw himself into the Danube.

I'll see you all tomorrow, God-willing. You won't receive this letter until after I get home now – I'll post it on the way to the station. I neglected to do it before, having been distracted of late.

Dawn will be up soon and I will be out of here at first light, even if I have to sit on the cold platform for hours yet before my train arrives. My nerves can take no more.

All my love

Alex

New Town

I woke up with the sun splitting my eyes like grapes bursting under a fist. Drowsiness fogged my thinking for a moment. Where the hell was I? The hard, thin plastic mattress and the fusty blanket over me soon brought me back to a sharp realisation. I was in a police cell. I'd been brought here last night. I groaned in despair as the memory returned in little jigsaw pieces, slowly slotting together. As the final piece slid into place, my stomach seized.

I remembered the copper marching me to the police car, and that helpless feeling that they were dismissing everything I said because I was a known piss-head and a 'homeless,' not worth taking seriously. They'd seen it all before after all, gibbering, hallucinating drunks trying to make excuses for their behaviour, being a pain in the arse and wasting police time.

But when I'd staggered out of the alley, shouting for help, it had not been the drink talking but sheer terror. And I was grateful they'd locked me safely in a cell away from the horror of the night, dreading the time when they'd let me go and I'd be out there again, alone, as darkness fell across the streets.

***

Those halcyon days after sixth form at school had ended, I can recall it all now as clear as glass. Nick, Jan and me driving around that summer in a battered Escort Mark 1, listening to The Clash, Siouxsie and the Banshees and the B52's on a battered cassette machine, passing spliffs between us, mocking the sheep walking the pavement in their mainstream clothes, pushing kids in their mainstream buggies, living pointless, mainstream suburban lives. All sucked in by the consumer crap that we're fed from birth. Be this, buy that, drink it all up and suck it down. We weren't going to end up like that, oh no. Not us. We would shine brightly and change the world.

Lazing down on the riverbank behind the sewage works, we'd watch the shadows of the tower blocks slowly lumbering along the bank opposite as the day passed and the sun inched around our world. We'd muse on life and what it all meant, while sharing a packet of cheap cigarettes. Sometimes spiky, punk

Tracey would join us, sacked from another casual shop job for turning up in a Sex Pistols T-shirt. "Screw it all!" she'd say and we'd laugh. She'd get another job, because there was always plenty of casual work about then.

There were hot summer days spent tripping on magic mushrooms and acid, wandering the green fairytale world that was Epping Forest. Or we'd lay out under the sky in the tangled grounds of a derelict mansion in the woods, talking lots of earnest crap about how we'd form a band, how we'd become existentialist artists, do something that *meant* something. Such plans we'd had, when we were marching with the crowd through the baking streets of London, waving 'Rock Against Racism' placards and jeering Thatcher and her neoliberal policies.

But where were we now? Nick had become a video shop manager, lured by his uncle's lucrative job offer, swapping bondage trousers for a shirt and tie. Tracey had just vanished into the churning sea that was London, and Jan? Well, she'd died the day before her twenty fourth birthday from a heroin overdose in some dirty squat in Leyton. Yeah, we'd lived lives that really meant something.

***

"Are you the same Jack Haynes that saved a kid from a fire back in 1992," the copper asked?

"Yeah. Some twat had set his flat alight. I was just passing, lucky really," I replied.

"You were hailed as quite the hero, I understand," he continued.

"Yeah, I guess." I shrugged.

Why did the coppers keep going over old stuff? I wanted them to ask about last night and what had happened then. After all, that's why I was here. PC Beaky shuffled through some paperwork on the table, his hawk's beak of a nose trying to sniff me out like a lurcher after a rabbit.

"You left school with quite a few qualifications, Jack. Went to art college. Worked as a publications assistant for SeeClear charity....so how did it come to this?"

"You mean how did I get to become a stinking bum," I replied dryly.

I watched the discomfort slip across his face. Yeah, say what you really mean, mate, I thought. But somehow I don't think Beaky was trying to get in a dig but maybe just get to grips with who I was, hopefully before he launched into questions about last night. I decided to play it cool, tell them what they wanted, show I wasn't quite the drink-fried brain-dead they probably expected to be dealing with this morning.

"Why am I wearing this crinkle jump suit?" I tried politely. "I never admired shell suits, even when they were the height of fashion."

Beaky took a moment before replying.

"We had to take the clothes you were wearing last night for forensics. Plus you'd pissed yourself."

Oh God! Pissed myself. I'd forgotten that. I'd been that scared.

"So, let's go over it again."

The other copper, who I'd nicknamed Smarmy in my head, was speaking now.

"You tell us you saw John Beamish when, suddenly, a monster appeared and ate him."

Sarky bastard. You weren't there, mate.

"Look, Jack," Beaky cut in, and I sensed he was trying to help me out a little. "You're not doing yourself any favours. Just tell us what really happened between you and Beamish. We know you weren't strangers to each other, and you'd both been drinking."

"I didn't hurt John," I protested. "I liked the guy. We'd bumped into each other over the years in various squats and drop-in programmes. He was a nice bloke. And I'm not a belligerent drunk either, not the sort that gets leery after a few. It happened as I stated."

But it sounded incredible, even to my own ears, so how could I expect anyone else to believe me?

Both the interviewing coppers gave up then and Smarmy took me back to my cell, leaving me with a plastic cup of coffee and some plastic-wrapped cheese and pickle sandwiches. Before locking the door he got his last dig in.

"You'll be lucky if you don't get charged with murder. Enjoy the condemned man's last meal."

I groaned and slumped on the bed. How had it come to this?

I started running the events of last night through my mind again. Foolish perhaps, but I was desperate to make sense of it all. I hadn't drunk much, just a four-pack of X-rated cider since lunchtime so I was hardly drunk, and then I'd spotted John walking across the square. I'd been sitting by the fountain. It was a typical new town square, surrounded by faceless office blocks, a Shoe Save, Iceland, phone shop. John had been walking, head down, shrivelled up into his brown mac like an old plodding tortoise. I'd known him even from that distance and had scrambled up to cross the empty square to meet him. I remember a crisp packet had blown against my arm as I'd stood. I'd almost expected tumbleweed to come bowling past, it was that deserted. Everything had been closed for the evening and new town centres can become desolate, almost eerie, places once the workers and shoppers have left for the day. I avoided the lively club and bar sector of an evening. Bums aren't welcome there. Doss down in a doorway and you're likely to get spat or pissed on, maybe even given a kicking by some brain-deads hunting for someone to take their frustrations out on.

"John." I'd called out.

He'd started, looked my way, his stubbly face splitting into a grin as he'd recognised me.

"Jack. How are y'?"

I knew John was in his early forties, a few years older than me, but he looked older than that, his face saggy and lined, his frame bent. His hair had thinned and grown since I'd last seen him and he wore it pulled back in a pony tail. Here was a former finance expert you'd go to for advice on your mortgage and investments. This man had knowledge, qualifications. Now he was just an anonymous bum, like the rest of us street homeless, faceless, avoided, judged, despised.

"What brings you here?" I'd asked.

"There's a new hostel opened up on Broad Street," he'd replied. "I heard it's easier to get beds there and the place I was at gave me a bus ticket to get here. Why are you here in this barren, godforsaken concrete carbuncle? I thought you loved London, good pickings you always said."

Some life had seeped back into John's bloodshot eyes and his voice had become more upbeat as we'd talked. We'd been genuinely chuffed to see each other. Walking the road can be a lonely life and John had been one of those fellow travellers I'd instantly clicked with, despite our different backgrounds.

"Nah," I'd replied. "I've had enough of it now, fancied a change. I've found a good spot around the centre here, lots of cafes, generous people. I do some cash-in-hand glass collecting for a wine bar on busy nights. There's lots of empty shops to kip in and the public loos are still smart, good for a wash and brush up. I'll stick here for a while I think."

"You still play your flute?"

"Yeah, got it right here." I'd tapped my rucksack, home in a bag.

Out of the corner of my eye I'd seen a young guy approaching. He'd drawn closer to us, walking quickly, head down. I remember he was wearing jeans and a striped green hoodie with the hood up, hiding his face. I'd thought nothing of it but suddenly he'd broken into a run and had pounced on John, pushing him to the ground. I remember not reacting for a second, being taken by surprise. Then John had started screaming. Shit, he's been stabbed, had been my first thought. The bloke was straddling John's body, biting his neck. I'm no fighting man and I admit I'd just panicked, looked desperately around for help, but the square was empty.

John had been making a weird moaning noise, his legs kicking. The guy on top of him had him pinned down and had started gnawing at his face. I'd made a frantic grab at the bloke's hood to pull his head away and then I'd seen what he'd done to John. Part of his face had gone, his exposed jawbone and teeth showing shockingly white against the gore and mush. That had been enough of a shock until this thug had twisted his head to snarl up at me.

The face had not been human, more reptilian. It had come to a short snout, alligator-like, with vicious, protruding teeth. The eyes had been tiny and yellow, glaring a challenge at me. A mask, I'd told myself, it has to be a mask. Then it had taken a side swipe at me, sending me flying. The rest of the head was bald, no ears, and scaly and browny green in colour. At that moment, I'd felt as though I'd been face to face with something infinitely evil and soulless, hollow. It had continued ripping at John's face with its needle-like teeth, ignoring me again, as though it instinctively knew I posed no real threat. John had stopped moving by then.

Call me a coward but complete terror had set in and I'd scrambled to my feet and fled. I'd run for the alley next to Iceland's car park, knowing that would lead me out to the main road where I was bound to come across people. In my blind panic though I'd run into the bin enclosure at first. Realising I was trapped in a dead end and that thing could be coming for me next, I'd become nearly hysterical as I'd backtracked and eventually burst out onto the main road.

A police car had been slowly patrolling past the shops and I'd desperately flagged it down. Events after that had got a little hazy once the adrenalin had seeped out of my system. The two cops had walked me back to the square, patiently listening to my garbled story. I don't think they'd believed me but were trying to calm me down and humour me while they checked things out. One had been walking ahead, talking on his radio. John's body had been dragged some yards from where I'd remembered it lying, a blood smear like a snail's trail staining the concrete paving. The thing had presumably fed and gone. The copper in front had shouted some expletives and I'd caught "his head is gone!" before I'd been cuffed and taken back to the squad car. There I'd sat shaking like a leaf in a storm while more police and an ambulance had arrived, the ambulance too late of course to help poor John.

***

My life had been great in my twenties, art college, more trips than you could shake a finger at, girls. I'd played in an experimental grunge band for a bit, nothing big, just local gigs around London. I'd been involved in the fringe arts scene, put on an exhibition in Hammersmith which had received good reviews. I'd lived on virtually nothing really then, scraping by in a shabby, shared house in the back end of Dulwich. But the pressing weight of modern society demanded that eventually I'd have to stop play-time and get a 'proper job' in order to get by.

And that's where it had all gone wrong for me. Some people deal with a break-down by medication, counselling, the support of their family and friends. Always a bit of a gypsy, I'd had none of that, and had cynically thought I could sort myself out, but that had failed. The slow bike ride downhill to crash at the bottom had taken over a year.

London had provided the ways and means to survive on the streets though. It had become a way of life, and one I'd come to embrace, taking pride in not claiming benefits but earning my small money from my flute-playing and odd, casual jobs. I'd grown to relish that freedom. I was beholden to no one, no one cared for me and I had no obligation to care for them. The rover's life meant no responsibilities, and when I'd had enough of one place there were no ties to stop me from just moving on.

***

There was no moving on now though. I'd been locked up for six days and the legal bloke they'd let me see had been pretty unhelpful, just told me they were going to hold me until the forensic results were back. Keys rattled in the cell door and it was Beaky who stuck his head round. Another ropey plastic cup of coffee, I guessed.

"Jack, we can let you go later this morning."

"What?" I was bolt upright on the bed at once. "You mean I'm not being charged with murder?"

"No," Beaky smiled weakly, as though relieved himself. "There was no DNA of yours on John Beamish's body and we found the hoodie nearby, covered in the victim's blood. It matched your description of what you said the assailant had been wearing. CCTV caught someone, matching that description, running across the square about the time you say the attack took place, but unfortunately the spot where you and Beamish were hit was just beyond camera cover."

"So I can go now?"

"Just some paperwork to complete. We recovered your tent and bag, with your flute still in it."

"Great. Thanks."

I could have hugged him. Two hours later I was walking out of the police station, blinking in the autumn sunlight. Beaky had given me a pack of sandwiches from the police station canteen and a list of hostels for the area. There were good people in this world, I mused, often where you'd least expect them, like a police station.

Then my thoughts turned to poor John. When the CCTV had caught a figure sprinting across the square, for all intents and purposes it had looked nothing more than a young guy in a stripey hoodie, not a monster. After all, I'd assumed it had just been some lad too at first sight, hadn't I? I'd decided this new town was not a good place. There was a taint here, something dirty, rank, unhealthy, amongst the gleaming concrete and pristine newly-planted flower beds. There was a disquieting underbelly muttering beneath the promise of the new estates and the shopping mall. I was soon on the road out of town, thumb out. When the lorry driver who stopped to pick me up asked where I was going I just replied,

"Anywhere out of here, mate. Wherever you're heading sounds good."

After some chat with the driver about this and that, I dozed off for a while, lulled to sleep by the monotonous rumbling of the truck and the dull scenery along the dual carriageway. I dreamed of John, me and him standing talking, as normal as day. He looked happy, radiant. I asked him in the dream if he knew what the thing was that had killed him. He replied he thought it was something ancient, something that could step through a doorway into our world when it pleased, take what it wanted and vanish again. I asked him if he'd suffered and said I was sorry I hadn't helped him. John shrugged in the dream, told me it was no problem and that he didn't blame me, that he'd have likely done the same thing and run himself.

"I'd had enough of life anyway. Maybe it was time to move on and maybe that thing did me a favour. Maybe it sensed that. I've found Shelley again and we're together now, as we were before the cancer took her away from me. It's wonderful."

There were tears of joy in John's eyes but then his tone became more serious.

"You need to be careful, Jack. Please promise me. That one got a sniff of you and it may be homing in on you now, as we speak. Don't hang around in lonely places. They pick people off when they think there's little chance of being seen and challenged.

They're very good at disguise. They can change their shape and give the appearance of being one of us, but they're crafty. There's lots more coming, I know that much, like a flock of birds that descend to feed in a field when the crop is ripe. I don't know how I know that, but I just saw awful images as it ate me, lots of them arriving all over the country. Keep an eye on the news. It'll start soon, mark my word, and there's nothing the authorities can do about it."

I awoke with a start as the driver beeped his horn. He'd slowed the lorry alongside a tall man on the side of the dual carriageway, a man wearing a striped hoodie with the hood up.

"Shit!" I gasped, John's warning from the dream freeze-drying me to the seat.

Then I realised it was just a normal guy, nodding and waving us on, phone glued to his ear as he paced beside a car with its hazard lights on. The lorry driver put his foot down and cranked up a gear.

"I always check in case they need help," he explained. "I broke down once and had left me bloody phone at home. Had to walk miles to a call box at two in the morning to get the RAC out. Bloody nightmare."

He dropped me at a junction near the business park in Maidstone where he was to make his delivery, and I set off in the direction he'd pointed, heading along the riverside path for the town centre. Town centres mean good pickings. The sun had dropped out of the sky and the last flush of the gold and pink sunset dusted the river Medway. Ducks called to each other as they settled in the reeds for the night. It was the sort of place I'd normally linger, maybe set up my tent and enjoy the peace, heat up some soup over a fire. But fingers of darkness were creeping into the sky now and I had no intention of being alone on this deserted path at night. Feeling uneasy, I picked up my pace.

Someone was following me, I realised after about fifteen minutes, walking that desolate path behind me. I glanced back, trying not to be obvious. It was a tall man, dressed in jeans and a dark top, wearing a baseball cap. He had his head down, hands shoved into his pockets. I walked faster, passing houseboats shifting on the river current, windows glowing with welcoming light. A thumping soundtrack and laughter drifted out of an open window on one boat and I could see shadow-people moving inside, smudges of colour behind the drawn blinds. I glanced back again and the man had gained on me. Was I just being paranoid? There seemed something just wrong about the figure, in the jerky way it moved. I felt oddly mesmerised and found myself staring, unable to take my eyes off it. Then I became aware of a slow mental paralysis creeping in, as though something were reaching out to smother me, to try and suck my willpower from me.

Alarm bells were ringing in my head now. Run, I told myself, run now! But somehow I couldn't. I felt like a deer caught in car headlights. But when the figure drew its hands out of its pockets and broke into a sprint, it seemed to snap the spell. I saw again the hoodie youth running and lunging at John. Everything about it now said this was some creature masquerading as human. It ran bent over like some scuttling insect and the arms were too long, not normal, not *human*. I didn't need to see more detail, I just fled.

The river path wound up to a quiet road and I vaulted a railing, lungs bursting, my back aching from the bouncing of my tent and rucksack. I could hear feet pounding behind me. Ahead I could see a row of local shops. Sanctuary. Oh God, no. Of course the shops would be closed for the evening. I pounded desperately on the door of the first one, a newsagents.

"Help me, please. Let me in!"

I looked back and the gangly figure was standing where the river path met the road, just beyond the reach of the streetlights, a shadow with long dangling stick arms, staring after me.

"Please!"

I was screaming in panic, unable to take my eyes off it. It didn't move. Why didn't it run at me, drag me back to the riverbank, do what it or its fellow had done to John?

Bricks. There were bricks stacked on the pavement. I'd almost tripped over the council roadworks sign. I grabbed one up, hefting it in my hand. Shaking, I smashed the shop window behind me and a window upstairs opened.

"Oi, you bleedin' nutter! I'm calling the police!"

"Yeah, you do that. Thanks." I yelled back.

Please let them lock me up, safely away from this treacherous world, I thought desperately.

The thing turned and sloped off into the shadows and I sank down on the pavement, clutching another brick to use as a weapon in case it came back. About five minutes later a police car pulled round the bend, siren off but blue light chasing, strobe-like, across the fronts of the shops. I was safe tonight but what about tomorrow, and the days after that? That prospect filled me with dread and who would believe a word? I recalled John's chilling warning from the dream.

"There's a lot more coming," he'd said.

The Bus to Texcatl

The heat was killing, a dry midday burner, and I realised I probably should have caught an earlier bus. I shared the seats at the terminal with a handful of Mayan women all bound, I gathered, for the next town, Texcatl, where I was also headed. Colourfully dressed in traditional costumes of crisp white blouses embroidered with ethnic designs, they spoke in a mixture of their own language and the local Spanish dialect. My grasp of Spanish was reasonable enough that I could follow most of what was discussed, and it seemed they were all bound for Texcatl market to sell their wares in preparation for the upcoming Day of the Dead festival. The baskets at their feet were stuffed full of decorated sugar skulls, paper figures of La Catrina (Mexico's Grande Dame of Death) and tiny papier mache models of leering skeletons in sombreros, smoking cigars and strumming guitars.

A teenage girl sat opposite me, her sullen expression in stark contrast to the rotund, chattering matriarch next to her, who I gathered was her mother. The girl wore jeans and a T-shirt sporting an American flag picked out in sequins, ironic considering she could never expect the same life opportunities as her counterpart in the States. That insidious hand had managed to make its mark on this young woman, all the same, with its glittery promises of aspiring to the great westernised consumer dream. She'd probably spent three month's savings she could barely afford on the prized little imitation FCUK shoulder bag she sported, desperate to live the dream in a one-chicken, dusty Mexican town. It struck me as desperately sad and I was glad I'd told the woman next to me that I was 'Englesa' when she'd asked which part of the States I was from. I was a white woman, so had to be an American. Where is England, she'd asked, wide-eyed? I'd tried to explain it was an island somewhere past France but her eyes had glazed over and she'd just nodded politely.

The bus came bouncing across the potholed square and we scrambled aboard, the women noisily stowing baskets under the seats. The teenage girl flopped down in the seat in front of me, across the aisle from her mother, who gave her a sharp look. I guessed she was making the trip under duress. I stashed my rucksack in the overhead rack and prepared for the two hour journey through the valley into the bordering state.

The bus gathered speed and the women settled down to chat. I tried to read my book but the scenery flashing past the window caught my attention as the bus left the dusty main town behind. We were heading now into spectacular mountain passes, vast blue skies pricked in the distance by an occasional puff of a cloud. At one point we crawled around the top of an incline with a steep drop on my right, which sent my heart bouncing nervously into my mouth. The driver was obviously an old hand at the route and we came out safely, picking up speed again as the road passed through small adobe settlements. Twisted, sun-baked scrub trees and the occasional tin shack advertising 'Refrescos' on battered hand-made signs slipped past in my peripheral vision, glimpses of lives so alien to my own South London upbringing. The bus passed a weather beaten old man and his pack-laden mule, then some barefoot kids playing football in a dusty clearing beside the road, engrossed in their game. I had a fleeting peek into the dark interior of a shack that someone called home, where pots boiled outside over an open fire beneath a battered lean-to. Then another shack, carefully painted in blue and orange, where an ancient portable TV chattered through the open doorway and spat flickering images into the faces of the figures taking a siesta inside. The tiny dirt yard was lovingly decorated with pots of bright flowers, hung out of the reach of the scratching chickens. All these images slipped by as if in an old cinema reel past my bus window, leaving an indelible impression on me.

But the one image that haunts me still to this day, and still has the power to make me shudder, was one that came about three quarters of the way through our journey. The dusty road had started to wind its way up a hillside, and the driver had slowed to take the bends. Suddenly the teenage girl sitting in front of me let out a piercing shriek and, a fraction of a second later, I saw what had alarmed her.

Walking beside the road on our side was a tall figure, unnaturally tall, over seven feet I'd hazard at a guess. It appeared human and male at first glance, striding along in a long, brightly coloured flared coat and purple velvet drainpipe trousers. It wasn't walking so much as stalking, the long legs appearing to bend backwards at the knee, like the legs of a stork or some wading bird. Those long, thin, stalking legs sported high-heeled cowboy boots, such as Mariachis wear for their Sunday performances, buckles shining and the carved leather lovingly oiled. Long chestnut hair flowed over the shoulders and it turned its face up to us as the bus crawled by. The slow pace of the bus afforded me several seconds to observe it. The face looked mask-like, pale skinned and gaunt. I couldn't see the eyes as they were shielded by the brim of the cowboy Stetson hat it wore, but I did note the mouth was a vivid red gash as though painted on by applying lipstick badly. All together it gave the impression of something completely out of place, some bizarre hybrid of a drag Mariachi and a New-Age Glastonbury festival-goer.

The teenager in front of me was sobbing hysterically now. The buzz of agitated voices from the seats behind us told me others had seen the figure too. A woman shouted out what I managed to translate as,

"Driver, in the name of Jesus don't stop! Please just drive on."

It was customary for long distance buses on these roads to stop and pick up people walking the road, or at least check to see if they were needing a ride. In the heat and miles from any settlement it had been known for people whose car had broken down to die of exposure in the worst extremes of the dry season.

The driver, maybe alarmed at the rising panic in his passengers, urged the bus up a gear and we left the tall, striding oddity fading into the distance, its shadow stretching across the road like an exclamation mark. Puzzled and curious, I knelt up on my seat to watch it through the back window until it was out of sight.

As I sat down again the girl's mother leant across and spoke sharply to her in her native Mayan dialect, and the girl suddenly turned to me in desperation, demanding tearfully in Spanish.

"You saw it too, didn't you? It wasn't my imagination! Please tell her. She didn't see it and doesn't believe me."

I managed to assure her in my best Spanish that, yes, I had seen the weird figure and so had other people on our side of the bus.

"Mama says I've got too much imagination, that I'm full of fantasies. But I know that thing was malo, something of the night and of el Diablo. I know. I see and I know things!"

The poor girl was distraught but I was at a loss for what to say in reply, so I just nodded and tried a weak smile to reassure her. In all honesty, the figure had disturbed me too and I really didn't know what to make of it.

The rest of the bus had settled down again but I couldn't reason to myself what I'd just seen. A carnival figure, someone walking on some kind of stilts so the legs moved so oddly, maybe practising for a Day of the Dead parade? But miles from anywhere on an empty road? And why had the figure alarmed me so, made my hackles rise as though I instinctively sensed I'd been in the presence of something malevolent and unnatural, something parading as human?

***

My old school friend, Reg, met me at the bus station and I was frankly relieved to get off that bus. The girl and her mother quickly vanished into the bus station crowd and I was glad there would be no follow up to the hysteria I'd been dragged into on the journey here. Reg, who was here teaching English at the secondary school, whisked me over to a taco stall which he promised sold the best tequila and salsa around. I desperately needed the first after that trip and, after catching up on news from home, I told him about the figure on the road. Reg, always sensible and dependable, chewed it over and then offered.

"Are you sure it wasn't just a bloke dressed-up, Jane?"

Suddenly it sounded really stupid, like I'd lost the plot and become wrapped up in some miasma of the superstition that had infected the bus.

"I know it sounds daft but there was just something odd about it. The knees bending backwards was plain weird. Look at that stilt walker over there. It moved nothing like he's doing, but that's the only explanation I can think of for its' height."

The pre-carnival excitement meant there were several people in costume already out in the bustling square, including a guy on stilts in the traditional La Catrina costume. Catrina always wore the huge feathered hat, lace gloves and aristocratic flounced dress favoured by upper class Mexican women in the last century. His black and white skull face paint (which had already cracked under his very human grin) took the sinister to just playful parody.

Reg grabbed my arm, steering me around steaming food stalls.

"Fancy a visit to the museum?"

That at least passed the rest of the afternoon, and as the evening drew on, candles were lit in windows around the square, heralding the first night of the festival. At last I managed to push the bus trip experience aside.

***

The following evening we were invited to take part in the Day of the Dead celebrations with the family Reg lodged with. I'd stayed in a nearby hotel, so to have a chance of experiencing this with real Mexican people was an opportunity not to turn down. Adorning the graves of dead relatives with bright flowers was touching and joyful, and the graveyard seemed to come alive with flickering candle light as the sun sank behind the trees. The perfume of copal incense filled the air as it smoked on top of the stones, welcoming lost loved ones back to symbolically share a glass of tequila. Later, the carnival procession through the town was as spectacular as I'd hoped and it seemed everyone had made some effort at a costume, from the highly dressed La Catrina stilt-walkers to children in their homemade skeleton masks. Marigold petals were strewn everywhere, smearing orange stains on the cobbles under the dancers' feet, and paper Mariachis and Catrinas bobbed from wrought iron lampposts in the cooling breeze.

Later we returned to the family house for a meal under the stars.

"According to Mayan mythology, Camazotz are the bat-like monsters encountered by the Maya hero twins, Hunahpu and Xbalanque, during their trials in the underworld of Xibalba," Reg explained as we sat at the table.

"Sounds like you've really been reading up on this stuff," I quipped.

Reg chuckled and continued enthusiastically.

"Yeah, I'm fascinated by the Mayan and Aztec cultures. According to the Popol Vuh, a demon called 'Sudden Bloodletter' is identified as one of four animal demons which slew the first race of men. There is a tradition of shape-shifting demons specific to this region, and some of the old folk swear they've had encounters with such beings."

"I never thought I'd find you into such arcane things," I remarked.

Reg shrugged and replied.

"Well, you can't live here, love the country and the people, and not really get into the whole history and mythology thing."

I was about to reply when our hostess started to tease Reg about scaring his guest with nonsense. She hadn't understood much of the conversation between us as we'd lapsed into English for ease, but had apparently caught the demon names. Conversation turned to other things and eventually I bid everyone goodnight at one in the morning, and set off to walk the three streets back to my hotel.

The streets were empty, apart from a couple of drunks in Mariachi costume staggering across the junction, laughing together. I suddenly had an urge to walk as quickly as possible, having the uneasy feeling I was being watched and possibly followed, and I almost bounded up the steps to the hotel foyer. Once inside my first floor room I chided myself a little on my reaction, but the unmistakable creeped-out feeling remained with me. The room was a little stuffy so I opened the window to let some night air stir the curtains as I slipped on my PJ's. Something was scuffling in the courtyard below and I leaned out curiously.

In the corner of the yard the family who owned this little hotel had set up a small Day of the Dead festival altar with the usual flowers and candles, which had now snuffed out. But they'd left the fairy lights strung along the fence on, and under their faint illumination I could make out an agouti, a sort of large guinea pig type rodent, scratching about in the flower bed below. As I watched his clownish scuttling I became aware of a figure standing in the corner of the yard in the shadow of a twisted vine that overhung the pergola. At first I assumed it was just a guest, standing outside for a quick cigarette, but then it stepped forward and I could make it out clearly under the moonlight and silvery glow of the fairy lights.

I say 'it' as the figure immediately struck me as not human, although it wore a La Catrina costume. The face was hidden under the brim of the huge floppy hat with a nodding ostrich feather. The long dress looked faded, rotten, torn, unlike the gay costumes so carefully stitched by the local women for the carnival. This struck me as the dress of a disintegrating bride from the grave. The lace at the cuffs was tattered and trailing. When it strode slowly into the middle of the courtyard I was horrified to see that the legs bent backwards at the knee, like the figure I'd seen on the road. As it moved, the knees pushed the dirty cream silk of the dress out behind it, and the shifting hem revealed clawed feet like a cockerel's, scratching menacingly at the cobbles. It lifted its head towards my window and I saw the red gash of the mouth under the moonlight, as though it had painted it on in some imitation of human lips. Its attempts at disguise though had just resulted in a hideous parody of a human being, and it carried an unwholesome air of something wrong, out of place, about it.

Something in my gut told me to close the window, get out of sight, and I instinctively did so, latching the window shut and jerking the curtains closed. My heart was pounding and I was afraid to look again. When I did gather the courage some ten minutes later the figure had gone and I thanked my stars I didn't have a room on the ground floor, where I may have heard it scratching during the night at the window. That it knew I was here and had sought me out I had no doubt.

Unable to sleep due to my nerves, at around three in the morning I heard the agouti again, snuffling around the flower bed, making its distinctive little chatter. Then there was a noise that froze my soul.

Another set of feet went scuttling across the yard, fast and with what I thought were accompanying claws scratching the cobbles as it ran. Then the poor agouti let out the most abominable shriek of pain and this was followed by a hideous cackle, as though whatever had grabbed it up was relishing its suffering. Next came the most horrible bone-crunching and slavering noise which reminded me of our old family dog with a juicy bone from the butchers. This went on for two or three minutes, then came another horrible, gibbering mutter before silence returned. Needless to say, I did not look out again and left the lamp on until dawn slipped pale fingers around the curtain rail.

I didn't mention any of this to Reg when I said goodbye in the morning. I just thanked the family for their hospitality and promised him I'd write when I was back in England. As I'd checked out I hadn't dared look in the hotel courtyard, just in case there was some evidence to confirm what I'd thought I'd heard last night, the chewed remains of the agouti - or a piece of old lace from a frilled graveyard sleeve.

***

The noise of the bus station and the crowd seemed a million miles away from last night's terrors. I found the queue for the Mitcaxu bus and waited in line. It was due in five minutes. I had to go back to the town I'd come from a couple of days ago in order to get a long distance bus overland to Oaxaca, then on to Mexico City to fly home in four days time. There in the line ahead of me was the girl and her mother who had travelled down with me. The girl turned, spotted me, and froze. I hadn't expected such an odd reaction but then she quickly looked away again and busied herself with the empty baskets. I guessed they must have sold their wares in the market and stayed over for the festival.

A moment later, I saw the teenager walking across to the burger stand in the corner of the station and then she was back, walking up the queue to her place at the front. As she passed me she gave an odd cry and tripped, sending the chocolate milkshake she was carrying all down my front. My shouted exclamation brought her mother running to see what had happened. The girl looked forlorn, and her mother chattered apologies to me in Spanish, turning to scold her daughter for her clumsiness. Realising I couldn't get on the bus for a two hour trip in this state

I headed for the ladies toilet with the intention of getting some clean clothes out of my rucksack to change into. My T-shirt was soaked and my skirt clung to my thighs with the sticky drink.

They both followed me, the mother still apologising and indicating she would go to the burger stand for a clean cloth to mop my clothes. To my surprise the girl grabbed my arm as soon as her mother was out of sight and urgently hissed under her breath,

"I had to do it."

Annoyed now I realised this had been a deliberate attack I was, however, silenced by the expression of utter misery on her face and the tears starting into her eyes.

"I can't let you get on the bus. I had to stop you," she continued. "None of us must get on that bus. I saw it in a dream last night. That thing we saw on the road, it's watching you and me and Mama. The other people who saw it too – it's marked them all. It's hunting us."

I just about managed to follow her desperate explanation and then her mother came bustling back. The girl now made a show of a fainting fit so her concerned Mama helped her onto a bench next to the hand drier. I understood the pretence and took the opportunity to dash for the toilet cubicle to change my clothes, concerned I'd miss the bus with this delay.

But that was exactly what she'd intended, wasn't it? I'd not forgotten my scare last night. Did I trust her 'vision'? I took out a fresh top and jeans, pulled them on, then stepped out of the cubicle, unsure what to do. The girl and her mother had gone. I went outside, back into the crowds of the bus station, but I couldn't see them anywhere.

The bus was just pulling out of the station. I'd missed it and the next one wasn't due until the early evening now. The best plan, I decided, was to wait it out and just wander the town for the rest of the day. I could transfer my ticket, so that wasn't a problem. Reg would have left for work now, but I was an old hand at amusing myself and so explored the craft market and the park. Shortly before the next bus was due, I stopped at a cafe bar nearby for some quesadillas and a coffee. The TV over the bar was showing a chattering soap full of dyed-blond Americanised women, pale-faced and dripping gold. One thing I'd noticed was that very few indigenous faces appeared in these shows, except as cooks and maids.

The advert break was suddenly interrupted by a news flash, a terrible accident I gathered. The pictures showed a bus upside down in the bottom of a ravine, and I thought the spot looked vaguely familiar, very much like the route I'd taken here through the valley. The words 'most of the passengers dead' hit me and the reporter went on to explain that the driver had swerved across the road for no known reason, according to survivors. Then a close up of the little yellow bus showed the name Mitcaxu on the destination board. Horrified, I realised it was the bus I should have been on. There it was, the windows smeared with gore from the poor passengers who'd been flung around inside as it had plummeted down the ravine. Many of those may well have been on the same bus that came here with me, visiting family and friends for the festival. Many of them would also have seen that thing on the road too, I realised, shaken.

The road block had been moved by the time my later bus took that same route round the mountain. One police car remained at the side of the road and our driver invoked the Saints aloud as he drove slowly past. I half expected to see the monster again, stalking the road in the twilight, and had horrible thoughts of the bus breaking down out here. But I made it safely back to Mitcaxu. When I left again the following morning on the overland Greyhound I couldn't have been happier. I often think of the girl with the visions, and am forever grateful to her and her chocolate milkshake.

Carousel

Walking home in the gathering darkness, Becky passed colourful posters for the Fair in shop windows. Every November it descended upon the common in a clanking convoy of trucks, and every year she and her work-mates looked forward to its arrival, a little buzz of excitement in the dark days before the sizzle of Christmas. 1965 would be no different.

"Let's go on the Big Wheel first, Becks," Nat tugged her arm as they approached the fairground, the smoke from her cigarette swirling around her face like a livid ghost under the neon perimeter lights. It was a chilly, wet Wednesday evening, and a light mist had descended across the Common.

"Damn this mud," Nat groaned. "I wish I'd worn my old shoes now."

"Well, I did say," Becky teased her light heartedly. Both young women giggled with anticipation as the pulse of the music drew closer, and the enticing smells of hot buttered popcorn and candyfloss drifted across from the gaudily lit stalls.

"Do you think that Nick will be here again this year, you know, the guy that ran the Helter Skelter last year?"

"And he'd still be too old for you and probably has a sweetheart in every town they pass through." Becky rolled her eyes at her red-haired friend.

She allowed Nat to steer her across the wet ground between the rides and stalls. The Big Wheel wasn't so big but she enjoyed the exhilarating view across the Common as their car reached the top under the star-less sky before plunging again, back down towards the lights and music, sending them shrieking. The chill air bit her face and crept its fingers under her petticoat, and Becky let her miseries slip away for those few moments, pretending she were somehow magically living another life. After the dodgems, which shook them into squeals of laughter as they rammed around the floor, and the obligatory candy floss, Nat insisted they look for the Helter Skelter to see if she could find Nick.

"He's probably moved on," Becky warned her. "You know how flighty these lads on the fairgrounds are, here today and all that."

"Yeah, gone tomorrow," Nat teased. "At least I got a kiss out of him last year."

Becky remembered, waiting awkwardly beside the ride entrance while Nat and the mysterious Nick fumbled quickly in the shadows behind her. Sometimes she wished she had Nat's boldness, her devil-may-care approach to life.

But Nick was not in evidence at the ride and the owner shrugged when Nat pressed him for more information.

"Sorry doll, don't remember no Nick."

Nat looked disappointed and Becky suggested they try the coconut shy to try and distract her.

"What coconut shy?"

"That funny old one there."

Becky pointed out the stand beneath a faded sign that appeared to lead into another section of the grounds, which read 'Prices' Original Travelling Carnival.' She couldn't recall this part from last year so guessed it was a new feature.

Compared to the modern 1960's rides with their thumping pop chart music, this side stall looked somehow out of place. It sat in a pool of dancing light cast by two torches in iron baskets, the wood board front declaring that this was 'Mr Ostlers Knock 'em

Down'. Becky guessed it was an attempt at a vintage stand, mimicking the originals she'd seen in pictures of the Victorian fair at the museum. Mr Ostler, in his Victorian-style top hat, suit and braces, was genial and welcoming, handing the young women their wooden balls for a surprisingly cheap hapenny a shot. Becky hefted hers but it was Nat who managed to floor a coconut.

"Well done, young miss. A grand shot."

Mr Ostler applauded heartily and handed her the coconut and a twist of blue paper containing half a dozen striped humbugs.

"Why doesn't he give prizes like teddy bears and scarves?" Nat seemed a bit disappointed as they walked away.

"Guess he's just trying to stay with the old fashioned theme. Quit moaning, at least you won something."

They were some way away now from the main fair ground, the noise of the rides fading behind them.

"Look, it's Nick."

Nat took off across the squelching ground after the striding figure of a young man, walking quickly through the shadows of a row of striped tents. Becky sighed, having no choice but to follow. The figure had vanished by the time she managed to catch up with Nat, so she tried to console her friend by suggesting they explore this side of the fairground while keeping an eye out for him at the same time.

Becky was curious about the stalls splayed out around them now. These were not brightly lit with coloured lightbulbs and neon strips, but loomed out of the darkness under brooding sulphurous yellow lamps that she took to be gas lamps. All the stalls were of the old fashioned sort and everyone here, not just the stallholders, wore Victorian clothing, the ladies in their long skirts, corsets and feathered hats, the men dressed like Mr Ostler. Even the children were dressed up, boys in sailor suits, girls in stockings and petticoats, clambering onto the rides with beaming, excited faces. She could only see one family in modern clothes who seemed to be confused, gazing around, and then they vanished out of sight into the gloom between two of the striped tents.

"This place is a bit creepy, Becks. What's with all the old fashioned stuff?"

But Becky was intrigued and pushed on forward.

"Don't be daft, this is like living history. Let's look around."

Becky pulled her reluctant friend between the stalls offering fried shrimp, toffee apples, hoop la, and pop-a-cork. A large steam-driven organ spat out plinky tunes as wooden clockwork figures rotated on top, a soldier and a sailor, hitting brass bells with tiny cudgels as they pirouetted above the organ pipes. Their staring painted faces were not jolly, nor welcoming, but somehow stern and forbidding.

"Ugh, creepy," Nat said. "What's that machine with all the belts and cogs rattling around, making it work?"

"It's a steam traction engine," Becky explained. "They were used to run the big rides like the carousel but there's not many working ones left now. There are pictures of them in the museum. I did a project on fairs for the last year of school."

The air here smelt of burning coal, engine oil and hot chestnuts.

"OK, great," Nat replied grimly. "But this is wrong somehow. Where's the normal punters? Even the people on the rides are wearing costumes."

They were now completely out of sight of the main modern fairground and, apart from the tinny tunes from the steam organ, no music penetrated here. The carousel though had caught Becky's eye with its brightly coloured and beautifully carved horses, shining under the gaslight.

"Come on, Nat. Don't you want a go on that? Then we'll go back to the modern rides."

The carousel manager stepped forward as they approached the ticket booth and swept his top hat off in a flourish. His face had a waxy pallor and his eyes flickered disconcertingly from side to side in a constant motion, like flies trapped in a room and looking for a way out.

"Welcome aboard, little ladies. Step this way for the ride of your life."

Nat clutched her friend's arm, whispering fearfully.

"Did you see his eyes?"

"He's probably just got some eye disorder. And don't stare, it's rude."

Seated on their horses, Nat relaxed a little and the carousel started up. On the horses in front of them a woman in a deep green velvet Victorian dress sat side saddle, next to a pretty girl with her honey-gold hair in braids, wearing buckled ankle boots and a petticoat embroidered with tiny roses. The woman bent close to the girl, whispering, and they giggled conspiratorially together. The lace veil of her hat obscured the woman's features, and she pushed a coil of wayward raven hair back up under the brim with a silk-gloved hand. She wore a sickly perfume that engulfed the friends as the carousel began to gather speed.

Becky's head swam under the combined influence of the perfume and scenery flashing by. The carousel spun, picking up speed and the plinking music wheezed with a renewed enthusiasm. *Let me off now*, Becky thought frantically, clutching white-knuckled to the pole as she struggled to focus on the carousel horse's golden, carved mane. The scene before her now changed. She saw the woman in green lying broken like a battered gull on a rocky beach, her hat gone, bloodied skirts and her loose black hair washing around her as the tide touched her gently, lifting and dropping her as it swept in and out.

The carousel wound down, and as the music faded away, so did the disturbing image in Becky's mind, melting away as she gathered her wits again.

"Becks, are you OK?" Nat peered closely at her white-faced friend, slumped over her horse.

"Yeah, I'm OK. Just feeling a bit sick."

Becky was helped down from the horse by the man with flickering eyes, who swept her up like a doll and took her into a side tent. A tumult of voices assaulted her ears.

"Where's my smelling salts?"

"Give her some air. Just loosen her stays and she'll be fine. It's just a swoon."

Confused, head swimming, Becky struggled to understand what was going on around her. That perfume was there again, sickly and invasive, intoxicating.

"Bring some water here, please, quickly."

The face close to hers, eyes full of concern, was the woman in the green dress. A soft gloved hand gently stroked her brow.

"Darling, I'm here. Come back to me, sweetheart."

"Mama," Becky managed after a minute, struggling to focus.

She was aware that this was not her mother but somehow it felt natural to call this woman by that name. Becky became vaguely aware that she was no longer wearing her tartan skirt and heels but black stockings, flat boots and a flounced petticoat, sewn with tiny rosebuds that came down past her calves. A flash of momentary confusion hit her but the mesmerising presence of the elegant, concerned woman in green soothed her senses. She was safe.

She was adored by the sweetest, most attentive mother in the world. It felt good to feel this after being unwanted, unloved, for so long.

As Mama gently lifted the glass of water to her lips, Becky smiled contentedly to herself. This was to be her new life, and her name was Marie-Anne Davenport.

***

"I need to get help," Nat shouted.

Something here about these people unnerved her and now Becky was hemmed in on all sides by the curious crowd. Nat made a move to get away and the carousel manager grabbed her roughly, his stinking breath by her ear.

"You ain't goin' nowhere, sweetheart."

She managed to wrench herself free, nearly losing her footing, and kicked him hard in the shin.

Nat ran in a blind panic for several minutes, fleeing between the tents, back towards the wheezing organ. Its jangling music seemed to mock her and she could hear the pursuing figures, their footfalls squelching in the mud.

"Stop that little bitch!"

It was the carousel manager's angry voice. A performing midget, like some sinister animated doll in frills, burst from a tent and scuttled after her. Then a costumed harlequin figure made a silent lunge from the shadows and she dodged, shrieking. Changing direction again, Nat spotted a figure on stilts stalking towards her, the painted white clown-face ghost-like in the gloom.

Her lungs rasped painfully for air, but the voices cursing her seemed further away now so she risked glancing back. Nat was relieved to see those chasing her had apparently given up. Instead they stood in a huddle glaring after her, picked out by the odd sulphurish lighting from the stalls, which somehow transformed them into horrible deformed shapes from some nightmare, all distended limbs and misshapen heads. She realised she'd just passed under the sign that read 'Prices' Original Travelling Carnival' by the coconut shy. It struck her then that maybe they couldn't pass that sign, some invisible barrier stopped them coming any further, and she was safe. Even so, she jogged on until she was staggering back into the warm glare of modern electric lights and the fug of thumping Motown music. Stopping to catch her breath again, Nat looked desperately around for help. Spotting a uniformed security guard nearby, talking to the vendor on the popcorn stand, she ran up to him.

"Please can you help me? I've lost my friend and these creepy people chased me."

"Creepy? Where was this, love?" He peered down at her, stubbly face a kaleidoscope of green, pink and orange under the carnival lights.

"Back there," Nat gasped. "In the old vintage part. Becky fainted and they took her into a tent. The carousel guy tried to grab me and stop me leaving. They were....weird. I'm scared of what will happen to Becky."

"Let's take a walk back and see if we can find her, shall we?" the security guard suggested.

Together they set off and he pushed her for more detail.

"So where did you go to find these old stalls? I wasn't aware there was a vintage part of the Fair."

"We went under the big sign by Mr Ostler's coconut shy, then found this organ thing and a carousel. We went on that and that's when Becky fainted."

They walked around the perimeter of the grounds twice but found no coconut shy, no Prices' sign entrance, and only the damp, dark Common brooding beyond the ring of modern electric light bulbs, strung along the temporary fencing. The mist had crept further onto the site by now and they seemed to be wading ankle deep in a ghost-substance as they searched.

"I think you maybe got confused about where you left your friend," the security man suggested kindly. "Maybe she's even gone home by now. But there's no stalls like you describe or folk dressed all up, I can assure you of that."

"I'm not confused. Look, here's the coconut and sweets I won at Ostlers's stall."

Nat rummaged desperately in her bag, where she was sure she'd put the coconut, intending to give it to her parents. It had gone. Nor were there any sweets in a wrap of paper.

"They were there. Honestly! I'm not making it up."

Tears of frustration and confusion prickled her eyes.

"OK, let's go to the missing person's tent so they can put out an alert for Becky," the security guard suggested.

Nat waited miserably for the staff to find her friend, but without success. They called the police and Nat gave them as clear descriptions as she could of all the people involved on the carousel, bearing in mind the fraught scene at the time. A police car dropped her home afterwards and she still felt they didn't believe her. Her tearful denials to her mother of drinking cider cut no ice either, and she even began to doubt herself what she'd seen, let alone explain what had happened to her best friend.

Nat dreamt of Becky that night, walking with the beautiful woman in the deep green dress along a blustery beach. Becky seemed younger, around fourteen, and was dressed in Victorian costume. They were laughing, chatting, bending down to pick up shells. Somehow the dream seemed a little too real for Nat's liking and something about it disturbed her deeply.

***

'Missing girl's body found on the Common' ran the headlines in the newspaper three days later.

Nat's mother suggested she stay off work that day.

"Poor lass. Just seventeen. What a waste," her mother sighed.

"But how did the police and the fairground security not find her that night? And they searched the fairground and the Common for hours the next day too." Nat sobbed. "And what about those weird people....there was something wrong about them. Why does no one believe me?"

"The police say there was no evidence of foul play, that she died of exposure, Nat."

Her mother passed her the *'Daily Herald,'* squeezing her arm consolingly. Nat read the swimming text through her tears, desperate to make some kind of sense of this.

Later that afternoon, she made her way to the museum, unsure why, but only convinced she should do after remembering Becky chatting on about old pictures there of the Fair going back over years. Becky had been quite the history boffin at school, and Nat wondered if she'd thrown herself so fiercely into her school work because she didn't have much of a home life. She felt that if she could find some answer at the museum that would be the least she could do for her friend.

Throughout that cold, November afternoon Nat managed to piece together an alarming, surreal backstory. Looking through black and white photo records of the Collumpshire area, she came across the pictures of the Fair in days gone by. There was a shot of the same carousel with its elegant horses that she was sure they'd ridden on, filled with smiling men and women. The credits claimed that the photo dated from 1898 and had been taken by a local portrait photographer. Studying the faces, Nat realised with a stab of horror that one of the carousel riders was the woman in green who had gone to Becky's aid, she was sure of it. And there she was again, standing beside the coconut shy, posing for the camera and smiling, a smile that somehow did not quite reach her dark eyes. Nat was sure she could make out the letters O S T L behind her on the front of the stall. The subject was listed as Mrs Felicity Davenport, Fairground Owner, dated 1898.

Fascinated, Nat sought the help of the museum assistant to find out more about the Davenports.

"There was quite a scandal about them apparently," the bright faced woman explained, obviously warming to her subject. "Mrs Davenport often travelled with the Fair, only settling down at home in Collumpshire when she married and became pregnant with her only child. All sorts of stories circulated about her dabbling with the occult, mistreating her fairground acts and with-holding wages. Many performers left her employment on a regular basis, complaining. We've lots of old newspaper entries too from 1899, claiming Felicity Davenport murdered her poor husband and fourteen year old daughter in order to inherit her husband's fortune and rid herself of the offspring that could also expose her crime."

She left Nat to read through the small file of clippings and photocopies. Mr Davenport had apparently inherited a considerable fortune from his banker father. The accounts claimed he was found brutally murdered in the hallway of their home. Mrs Davenport claimed an intruder had attacked him and he was duly buried, but not before their daughter, Marie-Anne, had whispered to the local Minister that she'd seen her mother stabbing her father with her own eyes. The girl was kept mysteriously secluded at home and allowed no contact with another living soul following this. Two months later Marie-Anne was dead from a 'withering disease.' A local doctor suspected her mother had quietly poisoned her but nothing could be proven.

Nat shuddered. The last entry in the folder was a death notification posted in the *'Herald'* that stated the body of Felicity Davenport had been found 'drowned and dashed on the rocks' on Collumpshire beach, apparently having fallen from the cliff.

"Or maybe you were pushed," Nat muttered to herself as she closed the file ready to return it to the front desk.

***

November 1966 brought the Fair back to town again. After the loss of her friend the previous year, Nat had no appetite to visit it, but Trish and Sal at the typing pool had persuaded her to go with them.

It was a blustery night and the rows of coloured bulbs along the perimeter fence bobbed and tossed back and forth with each squall. Crisp-dried leaves batted themselves against the chain link fence, as though desperate to get inside the grounds, and the savour of fried onions mixed with the burnt-toffee smell of candy floss in the air.

"Hey, let's try that new ride, the Spinning Octopus," Trish suggested. Once the ride attendant had secured them into boat No. 3, Sal started to chatter about her new boyfriend.

Trish's braying laugh, normally infectious, rode over Nat's head to become lost in the night as the ride started to move slowly forward. Nat had a rising feeling of dread pressing her stomach which was not the usual anticipation she felt as a ride gathered speed. This was something dark, almost suffocating.

The boat spun through the air, swinging out in an arc as the ride ran faster, so that they were passing over the perimeter fence below now. On the outside edge of the boat, Nat had a clear view of the Common beyond, pitch black and ominous. She could make out pin pricks of lights on the main road into town, the handful of cottages on the sea road to the coast. Then she spotted a large wooden sign just beyond the perimeter fence, and was sure she could read the weather-beaten name 'Price's' before the ride spun her away again.

A sick feeling crept through her as the boat went on swinging through its 360 degree cycle. Straining her neck as they came back round again, she could clearly make out the sign now. 'Price's Original Travelling Carnival,' glowing with its own sulphurous light behind the chain link. Beside it stood several silent figures, gazing in at the fairground but seemingly rooted to the spot. Nat was able to make out the tall figure of the stilt walker with the frightening white clown-face, and the midget in the frilled costume that had chased her that dreadful night she'd lost Becky.

As the boat came round again she was able to pick out the woman in the long bottle-green dress and lace-veiled hat, standing motionless, staring up at the Octopus ride, seemingly directly at her. The woman raised the veil of her hat and, just for a brief moment as their boat went skimming by, her face became that of a decrepit corpse under the carnival lights.

Nat's scream went un-noted by her companions, shrieking themselves with girlish excitement. The figures and the sign had gone by the time the ride came round again and Nat struggled to contain herself as the boat slid beside the mounting platform and the attendant unlatched their safety rail.

"You OK, Nat?" Trish laughed. "You're as white as a friggin' sheet, ain't she Sal?"

Sal nodded. "Maybe we should go round some of the stalls to let our stomach's settle a bit. Do you think there's a coconut shy?"

"No!" Nat burst out, startling them. "Please don't go to that Ostler's stand."

"What you on about, Nat?"

Nat brushed Trish's hand away and fled, aiming nowhere. Dodging around neon-lit stands, she finally slowed to a walk as the crowds around the hot dog stall blocked her path. Now she found herself walking beside the perimeter chain-link fence, gasping for breath and glancing fearfully out at the dark Common beyond.

"Nat, help me, please!"

She froze as she recognised Becky's voice, out there on the Common, calling her.

"Nat, I'm trapped. She won't let me go. I need your help.....please."

Shaking, Nat peered out into the darkness. A flutter of movement caught her eye, something that looked a lot like a tartan skirt and a red coat, floating and bobbing above the ground mist.

"You're dead, dead, dead," Nat groaned. "It can't be you. No."

"Nat, please."

Becky sounded further away now but Nat could still make out the red coat in the darkness. Searching along the chain link fence, Nat's desperate fingers found a loosely secured panel and she was able to push it aside and squeeze through the gap.

"Nat...Nat here..."

The beckoning voice sounded flat on the damp air and Nat stumbled on towards it, out onto the silent Common and into the darkness.

I Thought You'd Gone Forever

The hedgerows, spangled with nodding cow parsley and wild roses, blurred into one long smear of colour at the edges of Millie's vision as she pedalled her bike faster. 'Pick of the Pops' was due to start on the radio in ten minutes, and she hurtled as fast as she could along the Somerset lanes. To miss the pop show of the year would be almost criminal. All the girls at the factory would be talking about it tomorrow. 1962 was going to be her year, she was determined. This was her first job after finishing school and the pay wasn't bad, plus Bobby, the apprentice engineer, had even asked her on a date. She was sure this was going to be a proper romance, her first real boyfriend, although so far all they'd done was shyly hold hands at the cinema. She smiled coyly to herself, relishing the heat of the sun on her face and thighs as her skirt lifted and flapped in the wind caused by her own speed.

Sending pebbles spinning under her tyres, she pulled into the rutted driveway of the cottage and let her push bike slump against the garden wall, intent on dashing inside to turn the little Zenith radio to her show. Mum was usually busy doing sewing or cooking in the kitchen and sometimes came into the parlour to listen with her, but as she pushed open the back door she heard her mother sobbing, a sound that struck dread into her very marrow. Mum never cried, never made a fuss about anything, even after Dad had been laid off work and money had been tight. Hesitating in the middle of the kitchen floor, she realised the crying came from the parlour, and she could also make out a man's voice, mumbling. She crept to the door to listen.

"I'm so sorry to have to bring you this news, Mrs Gladmay. Is there a neighbour or friend I can ask to come and sit with you?"

Millie caught her mother's reply, barely a whisper.

"No, no I'll be fine. Really."

Her heart banging wildly, Millie crept into the parlour. Her mother, perched on the sofa, looked up, red–eyed from crying. The male voice had come from the local police constable, standing with his back to the window, looking awkward and out of place in their small pale green and rose-patterned room.

"Mum, what's happened?"

Something in her mother's crumpled posture and expression told her that whatever it was had to be really bad. Moving in to hug her mother, Millie wished the last two minutes since she'd stepped through the back door would magically go away. 'Pick of the Pops' was long forgotten.

"It's your Dad," her mother managed, swiping her eyes with the back of her hand. "He's gone, Mill."

"Gone where?"

"There was an accident......"

Millie felt herself struggling to take in this news, a sickening feeling creeping through her body.

"What happened, Mum?"

She looked desperately at the policeman as her mother crumpled into sobs once more, unable to speak.

"There was an accident in town," the policeman explained quietly. "A lorry ran into a queue of people at the bus stop and I'm afraid your father was one of those unfortunates that were hit."

He would have been waiting for the bus home after work, Millie realised. He'd only started at this new job a few weeks ago. No doubt he'd have been bringing sweets for them, maybe magazines, as was his usual habit on a Friday evening. Small treats he'd hand over as he grinned.

"Something nice for my girls."

The policeman made a move towards the door, his face tight as he glanced back at the distraught women.

"If you do need anything, Mrs Gladmay....The Coroner's office will be in touch."

***

The weeks after the funeral slipped by quietly. Some semblance of normality started to return to their lives. Millie noticed that Mum had stopped crying at night and had started taking care of her appearance again, curling her blonde hair into a sleek bob instead of just pinning it back behind her ears each morning with an old headband. That she took as a good sign. She'd understood how Mum felt, like she couldn't be bothered with life anymore now Dad was gone. She too had been racked with a misery she couldn't shake off at first, but the new girlfriends she'd made at the factory distracted her, and there was Bobby too, now her official boyfriend. The painful memories of what times had been like when Dad had been around had become fuzzy, bearable. She felt like she'd tucked those memories safely away in her treasure box, full of special things she took out occasionally to savour and cherish from time to time.

Mum had started listening to the radio more, now it was just the two of them. The little yellow Zenith transistor sat on the sideboard in the parlour and she and Mum would often listen to shows together, the Saturday afternoon detective thriller or a pop show in the evening. They hadn't done this much before and Millie thought it was great that Mum also liked the Kinks and Beatles, her favourite bands. Sharing these times with the radio was something they both enjoyed.

But the past couple of weeks she'd come home from work to find Mum shut away with the radio and the door closed. Mum would jump up from the sofa, flustered, when she burst into the room, and the radio would just be emitting hissing, white noise. Mum would seem embarrassed and would cross the room quickly to switch it off, making some excuse for the lost signal.

"It's weird," Millie told Bobby as they walked to the shops during lunch break. "I don't ever catch her listening to any programmes, she just listens to that hissing noise you get between stations. Sometimes I'm sure I hear her talking out loud, late at night when she thinks I've gone to bed, shut in there with the radio. Do you think she could be losing her mind?"

Bobby shrugged, trying to offer something helpful.

"Maybe she's still missing your dad and stressed out about money and stuff. People can do odd things when they're coping with pressure. Maybe you should have a chat with her, just mention it in passing and see how she reacts."

But Millie couldn't bring herself to challenge her mother over her odd behaviour. To do so would seem like she were admitting to herself a secret fear, that her mother was slowly unravelling following Dad's death after all, just as they'd reached a point of seeming peace and coping again.

***

Over the next couple of months, as autumn mists began to settle across the fields in the early morning, and the farmer began to gather in the cider apples from the orchard down the lane, Millie grew even more concerned at her mother's behaviour.

Mum had started taking the radio to her room at night and locking the door. At first Millie would hear a familiar radio station, music, the babble of a popular station host from a channel she'd last been listening to herself that evening. But this would suddenly stop and, through the thin wall that separated hers and Mum's bedrooms, that irritating constant static her mother seemed obsessed in listening to would creep once more. One night, unable to bear it any more, a curious Millie crept to her mother's bedroom door to listen and, above the grating hiss of the static, she distinctly heard her mother burst out, excitedly.

"Oh, of course. It's so good to speak to you again. I couldn't bear it if I thought you'd gone forever."

She thinks someone is talking to her through the radio, Millie realised with a sinking feeling of dread. Now she knew she had no choice but to confront this head-on.

***

The following morning was a Saturday and Millie came downstairs to find her mother busy at the sink, grating and squeezing lemons. She turned to greet her daughter brightly.

"I'm making lemonade, love. It was your Dad's favourite remember, that and my Victoria sponge."

Millie did remember, could picture them all out in the tiny cottage garden in summer, sipping homemade lemonade. Dad would get the deckchairs out and they'd all settle down with the cries of the swallows dipping overhead, in and out of the eaves of the roof. The memory stabbed her painfully, and she felt that Mum was somehow gathering herself up to announce something big. Sure enough, Mum turned to face her, wiping her lemon-sticky hands on her pinafore, took a deep breath and announced in a high, nervous voice.

"Millie, you might not believe this, but I've been speaking to Dad."

"What?"

Mum's eyes searched her daughter's face, seeking approval there.

"Dad? How?" Millie asked warily.

"I read a magazine article about spirit voices being able to come through on radio waves and decided to try it. It's called EVP by the Psychical Research Society, apparently. You find a wavelength on the radio that's not taken up by a station and they use the static to form words, the spirits, to speak. Here, sit down and we'll talk to him together."

Mum pulled out a chair from the kitchen table and pushed her teenage daughter into it. Then she rushed upstairs to get the radio. Her hands were shaking as she twiddled the dials to tune into the empty static hiss.

"Listen, Mill. You can ask him anything. He's still here, watching over us. I was so pleased when he first managed to get through. I'd been asking him to try for days."

Her mother was breathless with excitement, like a child opening presents on Christmas Day, and Millie's heart plunged as she was forced face to face with the reality of her mother's delusion.

For a moment there was nothing but the static buzzing frantically like wasps around the kitchen, and Millie sat rigidly in the chair, unsure whether to speak. Then a voice emerged from the buzzing hiss, an odd, slow, metallic voice that made her think of a robot or a synthetic alien voice from a sci-fi movie.

"Hello May, darling. And my sweetest Millie. How are you, Millie? Are you working hard at Jessop's, like a good girl?"

Shocked, Millie stared open-mouthed at the little radio with its dials and yellow casing, then across at her mother who sat in rapturous silence, gazing at it as if it were a holy object. But was this really Dad, or was it some cruel joke?

"Go on, love. Say hello to Dad."

Mum's eyes were big and shining as she faced her daughter across the table.

"Hi Dad. Is it nice where you are?" Millie ventured uneasily.

The metallic voice rattled enthusiastically back after a slight pause.

"It's very nice here, Millie. There are lovely gardens, full of shining angels."

Growing bolder, she asked.

"Have you seen Nanny Lewis on the other side?"

"Of course, Sweety. Nanny Lewis is standing next to me as I speak and sends her love."

Mum let out an angry gasp. Glaring at her daughter, she muttered.

"What sort of silly question is that? You know Nanny Lewis is still alive."

Millie felt overwhelmed but determined.

"If this is really my Dad, can you tell me when...."

"Take no notice, Dan." Her mother cut in sharply. "Millie is just upset and all this is a bit of a shock for her."

The static crackled for a second, like a cough caught up with a slow chuckle, before the voice continued from the speakers.

"Of course. It must be a little over-whelming. We'll speak again soon, Millie. Take care, and don't forget me, Sweety."

The radio returned to its dead-voice hiss and Millie fled to her room where she sat shaking, struggling to make sense of what had just happened.

***

That evening, Millie watched her mother silently climb the stairs, clutching the radio they'd once shared to break up the dull evenings, and then listened to her parents' bedroom door click shut. After a while, she gathered her courage to creep up the stairs and put her ear to the door.

First came the static, then that slow, rasping voice that had claimed to be her father.

"You're looking pretty today, May. But why aren't you wearing those shorter dresses I asked you to buy, the ones that show off your arse? You've got such a lovely, tight peach of an arse. Boy, I miss cradling that in my hands. Wear those lacy pants too, just for me, darling"

Millie cringed as she heard her mother giggle girlishly. The voice continued.

"Let me see it all, eh love. That peachy arse and tight pussy."

Millie leapt back from the door, shouting.

"Mum, that's not Dad! He'd never say such crude things. He never talked like that."

Her mother wrenched open the door, her face flushed, standing only in her satin slip.

"How would you know what he said to me in private, just between us?" She yelled back. "What would you know of what goes on between married couples?"

"Then why didn't he know Nanny Lewis is still alive?" Millie challenged angrily. "That's not Dad. I just know it."

Feeling sick, she fled from the cottage, grabbing her push bike from the front garden, and set off down the lanes, desperate to put as much distance as she could between herself and her mother, the mother she now resented for her gullibility. Finally out of breath, she slowed up and sat on a wall as the sunset spread gold and pink fingers across the sky. Struggling with her thoughts, she knew she couldn't dismiss it all as Mum's imagination as she'd heard the voice for herself. It had said her name, spoken to her personally. But there had been something perverse, threatening, about the tone of that voice tonight. Why was her mother so convinced it was Dad, her kind, quiet, almost shy father who would never use dirty words like 'pussy.' Millie was not so naive that she didn't know what that meant, how the older girls at the factory used it in conversations while they stood outside for a cigarette.

Plucking up courage, Millie cycled slowly home as the moon rose across the fields, dreading what she'd find when she got in. She spotted the radio sitting silently on the kitchen table as she stepped into the cottage, caught in a moonbeam streaming in through the window. Beside it was a scribbled note from Mum. She flicked on the dusty overhead light.

"I've gone to bed. Lock up when you read this. You can get your own supper."

She felt the anger in the words, and glanced warily at the radio as she made herself a cheese sandwich. Stealing another anxious glance at the radio as she passed it on her way upstairs, she half expected it to flare into life and that creepy voice to berate her for speaking up to her mother. Its slim green display remained unlit, but Millie imagined she felt it watching, brooding, waiting to pick its next moment.

***

To her relief, Mum had not come down for breakfast by the time she left to meet Bobby in town the following morning. Wandering in the park, Millie blurted out the whole sorry episode to him. He frowned.

"So you actually heard this voice too?"

"Yes, and it was horrible, gloating, making suggestions that mum should wear mini-skirts and lacy knickers. Mum never dressed like that when Dad was alive and he always said she looked lovely whatever she wore."

"Sounds really weird. Are you sure it wasn't someone pranking about, maybe someone living nearby who has a ham radio and has been watching you both? It would be pretty easy, I think, for someone to interrupt your radio reception and do that."

"The nearest neighbours are an old couple at the end of the lane, and whoever was doing the talking would have had to be able to see into the cottage in order to know what Mum was wearing. And how would they be able to hear what Mum was saying back?" Millie protested. "I don't think that's what's happening somehow. We live in the middle of nowhere. I can't see some malicious prankster going to the trouble of trekking all the way out there at all hours."

"Shall I come back with you on the bus, just to make sure everything is OK?" Bobby offered.

Millie hesitated before answering.

"No it's OK, thanks Bobby. I'll have to face her sometime."

She put off parting for as long as she could before catching the last bus home. At four o'clock, it was already getting dark and a bitter chill wind cut at her bare cheeks as she walked from the bus stop at the end of the lane to the cottage. Under the stormy sky, the old cottage looked foreboding and Millie was on edge as she stepped into the kitchen. It had occurred to her that perhaps the voice in the radio could really be something paranormal, but she was sure whatever it was had nothing to do with her Dad. Now she was in mental turmoil again about just how she could go about getting help for her mother and how she should approach her, if at all.

The place was in darkness, but the gloaming light picked out the yellow Zenith radio, still sitting in the middle of the table, which struck Millie as odd. Usually her mother would have shut herself away privately with it by now. She crept past it, and she did so it came to life with a gleeful static cackle, and the metallic voice of the airwaves rasped.

"Millie, dear. Where have you been? Daddy has been waiting for you."

She froze and stared at it. The green display glowed and it let out another hacking, mocking laugh.

"Why don't you want to talk to your poor, old Dad, Mills? Mummy still loves me. Oh yes, Mummy will do anything for me, even the naughty things I like to see."

"No!"

Millie fled up the stairs to thunder fists on her mother's bedroom door.

"Mum. That voice is on the radio again. It turned itself on. Mum....come out, please. I'm scared."

There was no answer and she burst into the bedroom. Her mother's still form was sprawled on the bed, dressed in the treasured silk dressing gown, covered in tiny roses, that her husband had bought her the previous Christmas.

"Mum, wake up."

Millie shook her mother's arm but it was stiff, and her flesh was cold through the silk of the gown sleeve. Her mother stared, unseeing, at the ceiling, the whites of her eyes a sickly yellow, and Millie spotted an empty bottle of paracetamol laying on the dresser. She could hear the radio mocking her from downstairs, the synthetic voice cackling up the stairs.

"Mum is with me now, Millie, here with your dear old Dad. What fun we'll have together now. Forever together, never to be parted. I made her promise me she'd drop by."

"Shut up!" Millie screamed. "You're not my Dad. You're evil."

Pounding back down the stairs, she grabbed the little Zenith up. It had fallen silent now, but the green glow of the display seemed to taunt her. Millie, sobbing, took it out into the garden and slammed it viciously onto the concrete path, smashing it to pieces. She finished what she'd started with the hammer from the shed, pounding the yellow casing and the internal workings to tiny shards of battered, twisted metal. When she'd finished she stood shaking, her tears staining the front of her blouse.

The Halloween Party

The crisp air bit at Jack's face as he walked up the driveway towards the old house. Its broad, sandstone frontage loomed out through the fine mist, giving it a melancholy, brooding appearance. Leaves, all shades of gold, red and copper, had been neatly raked into piles on the lawn, ready for composting. Orb web spiders stretched careful legs in their dew-spangled webs, slung between the rose bushes.

He recalled memories of childhood visits to this rambling Gloucestershire house. The smell of aniseed from fennel bread baking in the kitchen. Dusty old rooms at the top of the house, containing all manner of treasures to delight a young boy's overactive imagination. The old grandfather clock in the tiled hall and the portraits of distant ancestors that processed up the twisting staircase, stoic faces gazing out from the faded flock wallpaper. Of all the paintings of Della's ancestors, there was one he'd taken an instinctive dislike to. It was of her Great Great Grandfather, a stern, thin man, whose sharp face and piercing eyes suggested a spiteful temper, quick to anger. In the picture he was towering above his slight wife as she perched stiffly on a high back chair, skirts clutching her ankles in a classic Victorian pose. That painting had always fascinated but frightened him at the same time. The eyes had seemed to move, to follow him as he walked around the hall. Of course he'd never mentioned this to his school friend, Della, in case she'd laughed at him.

Then there had been that last Halloween party, when Jack was thirteen. He cast a wary glance at the old stable block as he passed the yard. The battered doors were closed, but he could still picture the interior with its empty stalls, and smell the dusty hay and dry, antique leather horse collars, even now. And he could still see that old horse-drawn hearse in his minds' eye, with its cracked black varnish, tarnished brass fittings and dull eye-socket coffin windows. The hearse had sat in the stables since the 1890's, unused, one of the many antiques that littered the house and grounds.

Friends and near-neighbours since childhood, he and Della were both twenty four now and Jack, a junior accountant in Cirencester, was staying nearby with his parents for a couple of nights. It seemed a good opportunity to catch up with Della, who was still living at the house with her parents, and he'd messaged her to check if it was OK to drop by.

It was Della that opened the door to him, dressed in jogging bottoms, a colourful Indian scarf wound around her head. Her dark eyes looked huge in her pale, narrow face.

"Hey, Jack. Come in, it's great to see you again. How are your mum and dad?"

"Fine thanks, but how are you doing?"

He knew about the cancer of course from Della's Facebook page, but the delicate, bald figure before him was shocking, all the same.

"Well, no hair now after the chemo, as you can see. Saves on shampoo and conditioner any way."

Her old mischievous sparkle of humour was still present though, which heartened Jack. He'd been secretly dreading the inevitable discussion of the 'C word.'

"When was the last time you were here?" Della led him through to the kitchen, where fresh coffee brewed on the Aga.

"That would have been Halloween of 2004. Funnily, I was thinking about it as I walked up here. Do you remember that awful thing in the barn, in that old hearse."

"Yeah, Dad got rid of the hearse after that," Della replied quietly as she poured coffee for them. Then she quickly changed the subject.

"How's the job in Cirencester going?"

***

The tantalising caramel smell of toffee apples cooling on the kitchen top, ready to be handed out by Della's mother, had been the first impression that had hit him that Halloween night as he arrived for the party. Jack also remembered sparklers in the frosty garden, and his six school friends trying to out-dare each other in the dark rooms of the old house. Della had won the apple bobbing contest. Then she'd suggested they gather in the front room to tell ghost stories. Jack remembered her turning down all the lights in the room so their expectant faces were lit only by two lamps and the snapping, popping log fire. They'd swapped tales, but it had been chirpy, raven-haired Della's that trumped them all.

"This is a true tale," she'd begun gravely. "And it happened in this house. My Great Great Grandfather Ebenezer, whose portrait still hangs in the hall, lost a lot of money on a bad investment many years ago and hung himself out in the stables. His poor wife found him dangling from a beam there. His last wish, which he'd left in his will, was to be embalmed and kept in the house for as long as his descendants owned it. So that's what they did. The family hearse out in the stable block brought his body back from the funeral parlour, which was one of the family businesses, and he was laid out in his best suit up in a room at the top of the house.

My Mum says she recalls Gran describing seeing it as a child, up in the attic room, like a shrivelled old apple, lying in the coffin on a trestle table. She said the eyes had been sewn shut and the skin on his face had shrunk so the teeth were bared in a horrible grin. The embalming hadn't been done very well and after some years the body started to smell and so they buried it in the family plot at Willow End cemetery."

There were mutterings of 'eww yuck' at that point, until Della, dark eyes shining with delight at the reaction, added the final horror touch.

"But Great Great Grandfather returned, determined not to leave his old home. Mum told me he was often seen in the house, a tall, thin figure dressed in the black morning suit they'd laid him out in, walking up the stairs to the attic or across the yard to the stables where he'd died. He hadn't been a nice man and he'd beaten his wife and children. Gran said his ghost would appear at the end of her bed at night and just stand glaring at her. Sometimes she'd wake screaming from a dream where old, leathery hands were trying to strangle her in her bed. So the family asked a priest to come in and bless the house. "

"Did it work?" Den, one of their school friends asked.

Della paused for effect as she surveyed her captive audience.

"For a while."

"Have you ever seen him?" Jack questioned, aware that Della, fond as he was of her, had a reputation for drama and spinning a tall tale. That had broken the spell and Della became a little defensive.

"No, Jack. I haven't. But I can show you all the hearse in the stables. You'll need to be quiet when we go down there. Mum and Dad don't really like me going in the stables."

Grabbing coats, they followed her outside.

"Shhh," Della hissed as they passed the living room window where her parents were watching TV.

Creeping across the frosty lawn with Della leading the way, armed with the torch from the kitchen cupboard, Jack wondered if this was such a good idea. The dark garden, no longer lit with the fire-dust of sparklers and the school friends' laughter, struck him as sinister, and the dark shape of the stable building against the moonlit sky, more menacing still.

Della pushed the crumbling wooden doors open and they stepped inside, joking and teasing each other.

"Ooooh," Den moaned. "I've come back from the grave."

They all giggled, shoving each other around into the old hay of the stalls. The family hadn't kept horses for years, and the stone and oak-beam outbuilding was instead filled with boxes of tools, dusty old furniture, and a sit-on mower.

"Whoa! Can we get the mower out?" Den crowed as the torch beam hit the shiny red lawn chewer.

But Della moved on towards the back of the building, calling over her shoulder.

"The hearse is over here."

They all followed her, picking their way carefully over the uneven stone floor. Della stood, her grinning face distorted by the torch beam into a leering gargoyle in a blue bobble hat. Moonlight seeping through a small window helped pick out the shape of the horse-drawn hearse and Della dramatically pointed her torch, like a spotlight on a stage, so they could all see it easily.

The hearse was covered in dust and cobwebs. The ancient paint and varnish had cracked with age and was peeling slowly, like the old dry skin of a mummy, while the brass lamps and harness fittings glowed dully in the light. It was Den who stepped forward to carefully open the back doors, revealing the dusty black satin drapes and the runners that had once held the caskets in place.

"Look at this," Den called to the others. "There's still blood in here."

Mike stepped forward and declared.

"Of course it's not, you knobhead. It's just rusty water stains, look, from the window rim."

Everyone grew a little bolder, peering in the windows. Della, showing off a little at her ultimate Halloween scare tableau, climbed up on the driver's box, where once the funeral parlour driver would have sat to guide the two black horses. Jack noticed Della jumped down quickly after a moment though, frowning and looking around, seeming a little agitated.

"What's up?" He asked. "Did you see something?"

"It felt like a hand grabbed my arm."
"But no one was on the box with you. We were all down here on the ground."

"Yeah," she muttered, obviously uneasy now, all bravado vanished. Then with false cheerfulness she called out.

"OK, let's get back to the house, c'mon everyone. Time for hot choccy, ginger biscuits and a spooky DVD."

Della and Jack were at the rear of the chattering party that headed back past the empty horse stalls for the main doors, and Della suddenly stopped dead with a gasp. Jack, nearest to her, asked.

"What's the matter?"

"It felt like someone grabbed my arm again."

Swinging the torch beam back the way they'd just come, they could see the hearse in the corner and Jack was sure he saw the drapes twitch. Clearly Della had seen it too as she focussed her torch beam on the windows of the coffin area, her face frozen.
"Can you see those white things?" She whispered.

Jack could. They looked like fingers, cold, deathly white fingers curling around the black drapes, slowly pulling them back. The torch beam lit up the face that rose to peer at them through the gap, a shrivelled, dried, skeletal face, the eyes sewn shut and the mouth a leering grimace of broken, yellowed teeth. Below the chin a stiff, dirty cream collar and a faded black bow tie became visible as the horror pressed against the glass.

Della's piercing scream alerted the others to turn round, and all at once panic broke out.

"Shit!" Den moaned, scrambling for the doors.

Della fled, the torch beam dancing madly over the walls as she stumbled, gasping, into the frosty night air. Jack was right on her heels, the others tumbling out after him.

"Tell me that was some freakin' joke, Della," Den gasped, coming to a stop halfway across the yard. "Tell me that was some fairground dummy or something you set up for our benefit."

But a terrified glance from a sobbing Della told him clearly it was not.

The commotion as they all burst into the kitchen brought Della's parents out.

"Dad, we saw him in the hearse....that horrible old man."

Della was shaking and crying and her father wordlessly took the torch from her and stomped down the garden towards the outbuildings.

"Look at your sleeve," said Della's mum, curiously pulling at the sleeve of her daughter's puffer jacket, turning it to get a better view.

Clearly marked on the left sleeve were a set of five fingerprints in a black, dusty substance, just as though someone had grabbed at Della, their hand circling her upper arm. Della let out a shriek and began struggling frantically out of her coat, throwing it down on the floor as though it had bitten her.

The whole story tumbled out as they sat down in the front room around the fire to explain to Della's mother what had happened. Her father returned a little while later, grim faced, and suggested they all try to forget it. It must have been something they'd all mistaken for a figure, he insisted, but Della shouted.

"No, Dad! We all saw it. It was Great Great Grandfather. He was in the hearse and he sat up and stared at us."

The party had ended abruptly after that. Parents were called, and Jack recalled standing in the massive oak-beam porch, shivering, as he waited for his parent's old Volvo to swing into the drive.

***

"So the hearse has gone then?" Jack asked, as Della refilled his coffee cup.

"Yeah," Della nodded. "It went the following week, sold to some collector of antique carriages halfway across the country. We watched them load it onto a truck and take it away."

"You never said at the time." Jack was curious.

Della shrugged, retying her scarf around her head. Her bald scalp looked painfully pale and vulnerable under the kitchen's strip light.

"I guess it had rattled me so much I just didn't want to talk about it, in case just mentioning his name made him come back again. They always say don't speak ill of the dead or they'll return to haunt you."

"You reckon your parents believed us then?"

"Yeah. Mum told me a couple of years later that they'd both seen Great Great Grandfather too on a couple of occasions but they didn't say as they didn't want to scare us kids any more than we already had been. Mum took his picture down too, just after they'd sold the hearse. She made some excuse that she'd taken it down to repair the frame, but it never went up again."

Later, on the way out, Jack curiously checked the hallway portraits and realised there was indeed a square of brighter, redder wallpaper. Della followed his gaze and responded.

"I never liked that picture, Great Great Grandma looked so uptight and miserable."

"No wonder with that nasty git as a husband. Blokes got away with treating their wives like property though, didn't they, back then?"

Jack felt a sudden flash of loathing towards the thin man in the painting.

"Let's not talk about him. He hasn't been seen for a while now," Della seemed suddenly uneasy. "Not since last December. Mum told me she saw him drifting across the lawn one night, towards the stables."

"No shit. That's scary. Well, look after y'self, Dell, and anything you need, just a chat even, please just call me."

"Thanks, Jack. I really appreciate that."

But they both knew Jack probably wouldn't be the first on her call list. They were no longer as close as they'd once been, as children, and this visit to the house had been on a whim after a long time of absence. 'Facebook friends' was the phrase that came to mind and it saddened Jack a little as he realised just how few of his old school mates he'd remained really close to, or had even stayed in contact with.

Trudging back down the drive, Jack pulled his collar up against the drizzle that had started. The morning mist had lifted but the fields beyond the boundary hedges had now taken on a dreary grey tone. It was a damp twenty minute walk back down the lanes to his parents' bungalow.

***

Jack was glad his small first floor flat in Cirencester was a long way from that place. The bright lights of the town were a welcome sanctuary after the dark, misty countryside of his childhood home. As a child, his imagination had often run riot, wondering what horrors lurked in those damp fields and woods once the light had left the sky and he was safely indoors in front of the TV.

The following night was Halloween and Jack made his way through the wandering ghouls and ghosts that drifted, chattering, down the High Street to various bars. After a few drinks with his work mates in a lively pub, Jack succumbed to home and bed. He dreamed, and it was not a comfortable one. He found himself standing at the bottom of a dusty flight of stairs that twisted up towards a panelled, wooden door, the sort that opened into an attic room. Something behind the door was whispering to him, calling him, but he resisted, afraid. When the door began to creak open, Jack awoke with a start.

Somehow, he felt the scene had been in Della's house, and the attic room was where her embalmed relative had been kept.

***

Della called him the following morning as he was making a coffee in the kitchen at work. After some chit chat about how great it had been to catch up again, she got round to what he felt she'd really called about. He detected a sudden uneasiness in her voice.

"Did anything odd, you know, weird, happen to you last night?"

"Well, I did have an unpleasant dream about going up to the attic of an old house. But that was probably brought on after talking about the Halloween party when we were kids. Why?"

Della hesitated before answering.

"I saw Great Great Grandfather last night."

"Oh my God. What happened? Was he in the house?"

"There was a tapping at my bedroom window. When I looked out I couldn't see anything at first as it was so dark. Then I saw a figure below in the garden. It moved towards the porch under my window and set off the outside security light."

"Did it look solid, like real?" Jack was amazed and uncomfortable to hear the distress in Della's voice.

"Yeah, he was solid-looking and he just stood staring up at me, as though he were taunting me. He had a skeletal face with skin stretched tight across the jaw and cheekbones, but the nose had collapsed and the eyelids had torn open. The eyes were milky orbs, like old pickled eggs. It was horrible. Mum came running when I ran onto the landing, screaming, but when we both looked out again, he'd gone."

Jack wasn't sure what to say, and he thought again of the creepy dream he'd had the previous night, on Halloween.

"Did your parents believe you?"

"Yeah," Della replied. "Both of them have seen him too in the past, remember? Mum wants to get a priest in again to bless the house, but it didn't really work last time. I think he just wants to stay and torment us. Maybe he thinks the family let him down by burying him in the graveyard in the end."

"I don't know what to say, Della. Maybe you should try getting a paranormal investigator in, or a psychic or something?"

"Yeah, maybe. I'll look into it."

"I'll come over if you need me. Do let me know how things go."

"Thanks Jack. I will. I'll speak to Mum and we'll have a think over what to do next."

Della rang off, leaving Jack to chew over what she'd said for the rest of the day.

That evening, he felt a growing unease as he made toast in the flat. The TV, burbling in the front room, proved no real distraction and he found himself going from room to room, switching on all the lights and checking wardrobes. When he went to bed, he lay awake for some time before drifting into a light sleep. He dreamed of leathery old hands clutching angrily at his throat and, when he awoke in his dark bedroom, he was sure he was not alone. The room seemed to have taken on a threatening atmosphere and was icy cold. Quickly switching on the bedside lamp, it seemed nothing was out of place at first, until he noticed the scratch marks on the lamp shade. Whatever had made them had dirty nails or claws. Jack couldn't reason that a cat had managed to get into the flat somehow, no windows having been left open.

The following day at work proved a distraction, but only mildly so. Alone in his flat again that evening, Jack began to feel uneasy once more, and the sensation of being watched was stronger, more insistent. He put off going to bed for as long as possible, and left the bedside lamp on when he did. Exhausted and unable to keep his eyes open any longer, he dreamed of climbing the stairs again to the attic room in Della's house. In front of him, the light of a lamp seeped under the worn old panel door onto the landing, and he could hear floorboards creaking inside the room, as though someone were walking about in there. Now he could hear slow, rasping breathing against the inside of the door, and what sounded like nails scratching, skittering, at the handle on the other side of the door. Something was trying to get out, to get to him. His own scream of terror woke him, bringing him back to the comfort of his own bedroom, lit by the glow of the bedside lamp.

Was it his imagination or were there odd marks on the grey striped coverlet? Jack leant over to examine them. The marks looked like a trail of black, sooty finger and palm-prints, as though two scrawny hands had moved over his bed, pressing closer to the pillow.

Della had once said not to speak ill of the dead or they'll return to haunt you. That had been her fear. Now Jack stared in horror at the hand prints on his bed clothes and his heart battered his ribs. Tonight, when he inevitably could hold back sleep no longer, he knew he would dream again. And this time he just knew the attic door would creak open.

Tiny Claws

It was craft market day and Yulia set out her bright-faced dolls on her fold-out table, then settled down in her canvas camping chair to wait. She watched Trev unpacking his van, the gold bracelets around his thick wrist catching the brittle morning sunlight. Yulia smiled. Trev was a bit of a chancer, always had some new 'gear' each month that he claimed was 'genuine antique' or 'hand-painted in Baroque Germany last century' or some such. Much of it was probably tat rummaged from car boot sales, she thought, but she enjoyed his company. The regular craft market stall-holders were starting to turn up now. Jane, who made chutneys and handmade greetings cards. Joe, the skinny young man with his velvet-lined trays of beautiful silver jewellery, lovingly crafted in his tiny rented studio. Sue, the funky pink-haired art student with her hand-painted T-shirts. The collapsible stalls were gradually laid out with an array of goods and the volume of chat went up as more crafters arrived, greeting each other and swapping news.

Yulia surveyed it all, wishing in a small way for a different life to this one. Perhaps she should go home, back to Russia. She'd considered this more than once recently, but wasn't this home now? It was all she knew, and what had she left in the old country? Her immediate family were all dead and gone like the snow in spring from the lowlands. Her husband had brought her here in the late 1960's, desperate for work and a better life. Following his death in a factory accident, Yulia had managed on her pension and the compensation money but, always prudent, she supplemented it now by selling her knitted dolls at the market on the Mall each month. They'd proven popular and even the brusquest Brummie women seemed to warm to them, stopping to break into smiles at their little knitted faces. Kids would watch, fascinated, as her needles clacked, rolling out a little miniature skirt or shoe as another doll took shape and came to life.

For Yulia, so long as someone spoke to her, noticed her, she felt that she was still a person with some value and that helped in some small way to salve her loneliness. She had no children and only one or two people she classed as real friends, Trev being one of them. One day for her was pretty much like another until market day came around again.

The Mall market was always busy. Dance music pounded out of the nearby *'Muzak Shack'* and shoppers scuttled in and out of the McDonalds opposite. Yulia watched them. After they'd fed enough on junk and slurped up bargains in *'Poundplace'* or *'Shoe Outlet'* she knew many would drift over towards the stalls, 'oohing' and 'ahhing' at the gifts and especially her dolls.

As she waited for customers, a movement on the wall behind her caught her eye. There was a lizard, not more than a hands-span long, dragging itself along the stones towards her. Yulia watched it, fascinated, and got out of her folding chair to peer more closely at the little creature. It wasn't really much to look at, greeny brown in colour, but its eyes were like tiny worlds, orbs of molten amber shot through with splashes of forest green. There was a little dried blood on its front left leg but it clung to the warm stone wall, bravely inching its way forward, bright eyes keen, long tongue flickering to test the air. She gently scooped it up. Apart from the bloody scrape the leg looked to be working fine. A vague image came to her mind as she gazed into its eyes, those inquisitive eyes made from opal, jade and stars, of a cat pouncing on this small guy as he lay sunning himself.

"You're hurt, I'll help you," she murmured to the lizard.

She felt its gratitude, sensed its relief at the trickle of water from her plastic bottle running down its throat.

"I will be well. I can heal so long as I rest in shade now. Thank you," she felt the lizard reply. Yulia put it into a small cake carton she'd found dropped on the walkway, and placed the box carefully on the table next to the dolls. He can rest in there, she thought. Trev had noticed her fussing over the carton and called over.

"What y' got there, Yulia?"

"A lizard," she replied. "He was on the wall. Look at his gorgeous eyes and his little feet."

She opened the carton so Trev could peep at the reptile.

"I don't reckon that's a native. Looks a bit exotic to me," he remarked. "Maybe it's escaped from that pet shop on the Mall. You know, the one where they sell snakes an' tarantulas an' stuff. There's lots of money to be made from exotics these days, apparently."

"Lots of exploitation too, with all the poor creatures neglected or just dumped once the novelty of having an exotic pet wears off," Sue commented cynically. "It's all wrong that some people use pets as a fashion accessory."

She'd come over to peer into the carton too, overhearing the exchange. Pushing back her shock of pink hair she smiled and added. "It's cute though. It almost looks like it's grinning up at us."

"What do you think I should do?" Yulia sighed.

"Maybe you should take him to the shop," Sue offered. "It's probably from there anyway and they have the set-up already to look after lizards."

Shoppers were beginning to crowd the stalls and Sue dodged back to her own table, sensing sales, calling back over her shoulder to Yulia.

"On second thoughts, if you want me to take him to the RSPCA on my way home it might be a better option. He'll get re-homed to an experienced owner who actually wants him then."

An animal rescue centre would be better, Yulia thought. That way he'd get a vetted home, not an idiot that would keep him in a tiny tank where he'd be miserable.

Yulia became aware of some teenagers nearby, five of them, two girls and three boys. They were all sniggering together, watching her. She recognised the faces as they often hung around the market, loud-mouthed, obnoxious and dead-eyed. Last market day they'd taunted her, shouting insults such as 'go home, scuzzy old witch'. Her accent had given away that she was not British-born, she'd guessed, but she'd ignored them and eventually they'd slunk away after some choice scolding from Trev.

The girls were cheap-looking and something about their collective aura made her think of dead flowers, a fading energy of something wilting, already spoilt, rotting. The boys were usually foul, spitting, leering, and swearing at passersby. She noticed several shoppers crossing to walk on the other pavement in order to avoid them.

As she found change for a customer, Yulia became aware that they'd slunk closer and she tensed, expecting some trouble. She wondered if they were drunk or high on something. Trev has also noticed and she saw him out of the corner of her eye visibly bristling as though psyching himself up for a confrontation. But the five of them started prowling around Sue's stall instead, the boys laughing, the girls goading her by calling her a 'pink-haired freak' and 'crusty punk slag'. Sue was not easily intimidated though, challenging them loudly.

"Haven't you got anything better to do than make a nuisance of yourselves, you bunch of sad assholes?"

Yulia didn't hear what the girl in the cheap blue stretch-top replied but Sue sneered, hands on hips.

"Yeah, bet you wouldn't dare say that if you were on your own without your pathetic little bully-gang behind you, you brainless twat!"

They seemed to back off then, wary of Sue standing her ground. This was obviously not the reaction they'd expected and it had thrown them a little. Yulia watched the stand-off curiously, wondering what they'd do next. Engrossed, she hadn't noticed the tallest, dark-haired boy until he was right in front of her, grabbing and rocking her flimsy table. Dolls went skittering across the ground, and then he shouted in her face.

"Go back to your own country. We don't want you here. Take your freaky pet with you, you mad old cow!"

The lizard's carton had fallen to the floor with the dolls and he stamped down hard on it, laughing.

Yulia shrieked in horror and then the yobs were running as Trev lunged after them, wielding a piece of broken pipe he used to wedge his van door open. Yulia barely registered much more than this though.

Trembling, she picked up the crushed box and steeled herself to look inside. The lizard was squashed, its guts spilling through its burst stomach, and its' beautiful opal and jade eyes were blank, staring. She sensed its life force fading away as a cloud in a blustery sky breaks and vanishes. Crying, she cradled the box.

"Yulia, are you OK, love?" Sue asked.

She nodded, shaking and tearful, unable to speak. Helping hands gathered her dolls from the pavement and Yulia packed up her stall, still trembling with shock. She tenderly wrapped the broken lizard in a handkerchief and tucked it into her coat pocket, intending to take it home to bury it. She felt that was the least she could do after promising to take care of it.

Trev returned some minutes later and to a spontaneous round of applause from the stall holders and shoppers who had witnessed the horrible scene.

"Come on, Yulia. I'll drive you home. Sue can watch my stall," he offered quietly.

She gratefully accepted, letting him help her into the passenger seat of his battered van.

"Did you catch the boy?"

Yulia managed to speak at last as they crossed the Bush Hill roundabout.

"Fat chance," Trev chuckled. "He outran me – not as fit as I once was – but I don't think that little bastard will be coming back somehow. I've reported the incident to the police and I reckon they're on CCTV all the way through the Mall."

As the afternoon sun slid behind a bank of storm cloud, Yulia dug a small hole beneath the laurel bush in her back garden and placed the cold, broken lizard's body into it. She paused for a moment to admire its smooth skin, its tiny perfect toes and claws. 'What harm did you do to anyone that such a monster should be so cruel to you,' she thought? 'So mindless as to stamp your life out.'

She gazed at the little grave as the rain started to spit down, sending her back into the house. Picking up her knitting bag from the table, she silently wished something, some powerful overseeing entity, some god with a sword of justice, would appear and wreak revenge on behalf of the small being she'd just buried. Knitting always proved to be a comfort for

Yulia in times of stress and, as she brooded over the cruel death of the lizard, her needles clacked distractedly. Scowling, she knitted a tiny figure, barely registering choosing the colour of the wool. As the knitting needles clacked, the doll took shape as though it had a life of its own. After twenty minutes Yulia stopped and looked at what she'd created.

"Oh, but you *are* an ugly one. I couldn't sell you on my stall. You'd scare the kids."

She chuckled at the brown, naked, six inch tall figure. It was a human shape but the arms were too long and it had no neck, giving it a troll-like appearance. Obviously, she hadn't really been thinking and paying attention to what her hands had been doing, had just knitted in autopilot.

"I'll have to give you a face to match, in that case."

She light-heartedly picked up a needle already threaded with black wool. Moments later the figure had a face, the mouth a slash of red wool, the eyes little black knots. It was nothing like her usual cheerful boys and girls with their little pink smiles and blue button eyes.

"I'll call you Narlia," Yulia stated, stuffing the little figure with a wad of cotton gauze before neatly sewing up the back seam. "Maybe you can represent the god of small animals and watch over them."

As a child on the Russian Steppes, Yulia had often seen the spirit of the land, moving through the landscape. In the winter he'd appear like a freezing breath that faded quickly on the air, flitting through the trees as she picked up firewood behind her home. In summer he would rustle the barley heads in the fields, moving like an unseen hand running gently and lovingly across the crop. She'd been scared the first time she'd encountered him and had run back to the house, crying. Then she'd sat down and reasoned to herself that this being hadn't hurt her, so why be afraid? That he'd allowed her to see him must mean she was special. When the spirit had started to whisper good things in her ear she'd felt privileged, chosen.

On the Solstice she and Grandma would light a candle for the lord of the land, knowing he would appreciate the gesture. He had a different face for each season, Grandma had said. In winter he bore a beard made of the hoar frost that painted the trees and fences white. In summer he danced in his greenery, running wild across the grassland below the mountains. Come autumn he was wrapped in a cloak of mist and reddening leaves, and his spring self was a virile young man who had hair spun with the gold of new buttercups.

Yulia's mother had not believed her when she'd told of what she'd seen, and had scolded her for believing Grandma's tales.

"Take no notice of her stories. It's just old Pagan fairytales and superstition," she'd said. "No wonder the villagers around here call her a witch."

Yulia sighed. Those memories of her youth now seemed unreal and dreamlike, almost from another world. There was no lord of the land in this grimy, concrete-bound Birmingham suburb. How could he run the streets and make the pavements ripple with delight as he passed?

"Call me an old fool," Yulia murmured aloud, gazing at the doll. "But sometimes it would be nice to believe in such things again with the passion I had then."

On a sudden impulse she didn't understand herself, she muttered under her breath.

"Lord of the fields, eye of the land, please bring justice and right a wrong. I ask for the little scaled one."

Grandma had used similar words in invocations to the spirits, and they somehow slipped naturally from her tongue. The air in the middle of the room seemed to shimmer as though there were a gossamer-thin veil of spangled material being shaken before her eyes. She was still able to see the furniture and the furthest wall through the shimmer, but it was thickening, becoming more solid. Then it vanished. She let out a gasp of amazement. Did something, somewhere, understand and was answering her request? As a child she would not have questioned the reality of the experience, but here she was, an adult in a modern city where the only place bogeymen and nature spirits existed was surely in story books?

"No, you're letting your imagination get the better of you, just as you did when you thought the lizard spoke to you," Yulia scolded herself.

Quickly, maybe even a little uneasily, she placed the woollen troll-figure on the mantelpiece. Then she headed for the kitchen, intent on fixing a cheese and beetroot sandwich.

***

On the Sunday following the lizard incident, Yulia walked to the nearby park. It wasn't much more than a strip of woods leading down to some playing fields and the canal, which hosted more rubbish than wildlife. She bought a coffee from the small cafe by the car park, and found an empty picnic bench.

The sound of crockery smashing and the angry voice of the cafe owner, carrying across on the autumn air, caught Yulia's attention. Two youths came running out of the shack, hooting and shrieking with laughter, and vanished down the path into the trees. Her heart skipped and sank as she recognised them, the vile girl that had sworn at Sue at the market and the thug who had stamped on the lizard. Seeing that cocky, sneering face again brought that day painfully back to her. Today though, instead of fear, she felt pure loathing for these individuals. All the contempt she'd ever felt for all those who'd hurt her during her life came welling up, bursting forth like a pressure cooker blowing. Her scornful, cold mother. Her impotent, selfish husband. She glared after the retreating youths, tears springing to her eyes as she pictured that innocent crushed lizard again, and wished them every ill in the world, that every wrong they'd done to another would come back on them three-fold.

She noticed the air in front of her seemed to shimmer, as it had done in her front room after she'd named the doll. She was still able to see the sunlit car park and the trees beyond the rippling, but it was thickening, becoming more tangible. She clasped her hand to her mouth.

The place seemed suddenly unnaturally silent, no excited dogs barking, no birds singing, just a flat silence as though time had become oddly suspended. It lasted for a moment or two, then all was back to normal, and Yulia found herself staring away at the trees as though in a trance. A little unnerved, she wiped her hands and face with a tissue from her bag. Her coffee had gone cold. The sun had vanished and a stiff breeze tugged a handful of fallen leaves across the car park. By the time she arrived home, lights were appearing in the windows down her street and she felt oddly elated as she opened the front door. Deep down in her gut she knew something monumental was about to take place, something she was a part of.

***

Yulia sat down the following morning as she always did to catch the local TV news before starting her household chores. She turned the volume up to catch the newsreader's monotone voice better. The headline story shook her to her toes – two teenagers found dead beside the canal. The photos of the victims flashed up on screen and she recognised the bully-girl and the thug who'd stamped on her lizard.

The girl had apparently been strangled and had suffered massive crush injuries to her throat, the newsreader stated. The teenage lad had suffered the worst injuries however, his ribcage crushed as if by a huge weight, and his body covered with tiny razor cuts. The newsreader stated that the police were blaming the attacks on a rival gang off the Hemland estate.

Despite her horror, Yulia found herself feeling a little justified, and muttered aloud.

"As you sow, so shall you reap. Witch you called me. Well maybe I am."

But what exactly had she invited in? Yulia felt a chill of doubt creeping in now. Grandma had always said be mindful of thoughts and desires as they weave the fabric of the universe around you, moulding reality on a subtle, unseen level like clay fashioned by your hands. Darkly things from other realities may be listening in, attracted by wild emotions and negative thoughts, just waiting for their moment to step through, to take advantage.

But even if such a thing could happen, revenge wreaked remotely by supernatural forces, why had she dared suppose she could be the agent of that? No, she decided, there would be an explanation and the crime would be solved.

As the smugness left her she felt saddened, ashamed of herself for ill-wishing the young people. What torment would their families be going through? No one deserved that no matter what they'd done, she reasoned. They'd just been stupid kids who'd known no better, had probably come from families where they'd never been taught right from wrong, so what hope had they from the start? And the shimmering shape had been a trick of the light, she told herself firmly, just her old eyes and over-active imagination.

That evening she cooked herself borsch and went through her usual routine of locking up. The shadows in the hall seemed unusually dense tonight as Yulia climbed the stairs. She left her bedside lamp on when she retired, feeling uneasy, although she didn't know why. Noises on the landing stirred her from a light sleep a little after midnight, but she dared not open the bedroom door to check, fearful she may come face to face with the blood-soaked ghosts of those youths.

"Too much silly imagination," she scolded herself aloud. "Probably next door's cat snuck in again while the back window was open."

But no, there it was again. A dragging and padding sound, of something heavy making its way across the floorboards. It was outside her bedroom now, the sound of claws scratching on the panelling, loud and unmistakable. Yulia scrambled out of bed, determined to catch the cat she was sure was the maker of the noise. Flinging open the bedroom door she flicked on the landing light.

A misty, dark mass was hanging in the air by the banisters. It seemed alive, pulsating slightly, as though it were breathing. It hung there just for a few seconds before it dissipated and vanished. Stifling a scream, she ran back into the bedroom and slammed a chair under the door handle.

'If I created it somehow, or brought it here, then I can un-make it or send it back from where it came,'

Yulia thought determinedly. But there were no more noises that night.

Her little knitted troll figure caught her eye when she went downstairs the next morning, sitting attentively on the mantelpiece in a shaft of autumn sunlight. Peering closely at it, she was sure it had long nails on its hands, nails she'd not put there. Picking it up, she realised they were loose cotton threads from where she'd sewn it up, but all the same it made her wonder. She normally trimmed all loose threads off neatly.

"Oh well, I was a bit upset that day," she said aloud. "I must have been distracted. But it does look like you have tiny claws, my man."

Putting the doll back on the mantelpiece she thought no more about it.

***

Yulia usually organised a lift to the market with Trev, and he was puzzled that he hadn't heard from her in two weeks. When she didn't answer her phone either he became concerned. Yulia was far from a frail pensioner. Quite the opposite, in fact. She was fairly robust for her age which made Trev all the more worried something bad had happened to her. On impulse he drove past her home and knocked on the door. There was no answer. Trying the back door, the market trader was alarmed to see the elderly woman lying on the floor in the hallway beyond the kitchen. The glass smashed easily under his elbow and Trev was inside. The smell of decomposition instantly hit him in the face, sending him retching, and it was obvious nothing could be done for Yulia. Before the ambulance took her body away, Trev noted something odd and remarked to the ambulance man.

"Those tiny gashes all over her face and arms, do you reckon a cat could have attacked her?"

"I think it's a straight-forward heart attack from what I can see. Maybe a cat had a go at her as she lay there, I guess," the other replied

Then Trev realised that Yulia didn't have a cat, or any other pets.

***

Yulia had cried and wailed in vain as the police, ambulance crew and Trev had left, but she'd realised by now of course no one could see or hear her.

She'd clutched at Trev's arm in desperation, had tugged the shirt of the ambulance man. He'd glanced up as though aware of something touching him, but had looked right through her as though she were invisible.

"Please, someone help me. Please!"

She'd fled upstairs and slumped in despair on her bed once they'd gone. The fact that she was dead had not really concerned her after the initial shock. 'Who will miss me,' she'd thought cynically? But then the full terrifying realisation had hit her, that she'd not passed over into some afterlife, but was trapped in her own home with that thing she'd called through. She'd tried to flee the house of course, banging windows, rattling frantically at the door handles with no effect. She'd even thrown herself at the back door in the hope she'd pass through it. After all, ghosts were supposed to be able to do that, she'd reasoned. But something held her here, stopped her moving on to wherever she was supposed to go to next, as though she were suspended in a soap bubble inside the house.

During the days that followed, she wandered aimlessly from room to room, watching the dust gather. The cuckoo clock on the living room wall had run down. In a mad bid for things to be right, familiar, Yulia had even tried to rewind it, just to hear its' comforting tocking again. Of course her desperate fingers lacked earthly substance and had simply passed through the key, so the clock remained silent. The little knitted doll stared silently from the mantelpiece and she avoided looking at it or walking past it. It was now an object of fear and loathing for her.

It had started shortly after her passing. Come dusk, the little troll would slip down off the mantelpiece and, whichever room she was hiding in, it would find her. It would scramble up onto her shoulder, twist its tiny claws in her hair and taunt her in its hissing voice, whispering obscenities. She would scream, flee from room to room, pursued by her tormentor until dawn, when it would return to its mantelpiece. She knew for sure now that this was not any benevolent spirit that looked after small animals, but a horror her own misdirected will had invited in to animate this tiny, woollen figure.

Yulia watched the season changing in her garden. As the sunset painted a golden glow across the windows of the houses opposite, setting them on fire, she would see the woman in the house behind hers draw her curtains against the gathering night.

'I'm invisible to you too,' she thought. 'I'm trapped and no one can help me.'

In her garden, birds settled for the night in the laurel bush, above the tiny lizard's grave.

The Sideways Dancing Woman

The taxi drew up at the gates of Adoracion House and Ben stepped out. The full weight of the Spanish midday heat hit him like a boxers' fist as he left the air conditioned Peugeot.

"Thanks, keep the change."

The taxi driver nodded and Ben hefted his rucksack onto the verge, the first beads of sweat bursting on his brow. As the taxi vanished down the country road in a cloud of dust, he drank in the first sounds and smells of the Spanish countryside. Crickets rasped in the fields beside the road, and the dry, still air caressed him with the perfumes of sun-baked oranges and cedar trees. Ben took a moment to absorb the view, fields of corn, fruit and nut orchards, a patchwork of yellow, ochres and lush greens stretching away towards the pastel chalk blue smudge of the hills. 'I get it now', he thought. 'I really get why she loved this place so much, and why she never tired of painting and sketching it all. It really is magical.'

The farmhouse sprawled around a verdant courtyard, its walls brimming with faded terracotta pots spilling with geraniums. Squat, built of soft gold stone, it seemed to doze in the midday heat, windows shuttered with blinds like half closed eyes.

"Hello?"

Ben called through the open front door, suddenly ashamed that he knew no Spanish, despite having been married to a fluent Spanish-speaking art teacher for many years. He fumbled the phrase book from his shirt pocket and tried again.

"Er, hola."

There were shuffling movements in the shadows within, and a middle aged Spanish woman came bustling out, her face breaking into a bright, gappy smile.

"Hola, Senor. I am Adela, the cook. You are first to arrive. Please come in and I show you your room. Meester Tony will arrive this evening from Gerona."

"That's our tutor?"

"'Ee is, Senor."

Following Adela inside, the sudden shade of the interior confused Ben's vision for a few seconds, until his eyes adjusted.

"Wow. Fantastic building," he offered, as he took in the bare stone flag floors, rustic furniture and open stone fireplace of the wide hall.

"It is," Adela replied proudly. "Very old, sixteenth century. Kitchens are through here, so please treat it like your home and help yourself to cold drinks and snacks, I think you say. We're very informal, not like a hotel, si?"

That beaming Spanish smile again, and Ben started to feel more at ease.

His room was on the first floor at the back of the building, overlooking the gardens, and Adela called over her shoulder as she left him to settle in.

"Come down when you are ready, Senor. I will be cooking for tonight, but please explore gardens. We have nice walks and a pool."

The gardens were delightful, he discovered, and he followed a walkway bordered by tall cypress trees down to the orchard. The path led through herb and flower beds, past a sparkling cherub fountain and a twisted olive tree which poked bleached, wood-fingers at the sky. Behind the left wing of the house he found the open air swimming pool, the turquoise water disturbed only by the sprinkler that kissed the lawn and the edge of the pool. He was just debating whether to take a dip, when a commotion of voices and slamming car doors, drifting back from the house, told him his fellow painting break holiday-makers must had arrived.

***

Over dinner that evening the would-be painters introduced themselves properly.

"Well, this is supposed to be a chance for John and I to find a hobby we can share." Iris, bubbly and middle aged from Bolton, announced. "He's either fishing or doing whatever men do in their sheds, so we thought we'd try this. It's very different to our usual holidays in Majorca."

"I reckon my artistic skill is around stick men level, but I promised I'd give it a go." Her walrus-like husband grinned. "What's your job, Ben, if I may ask?"

"Sure," Ben replied. "I just manage my local branch of Isla supermarkets, bit of a desk job really. This is totally new for me too."

The rest of the group comprised of Jo and Abby, both graphic designers in their twenties from London, and Ingrid and Helgi, two retired teachers from

Sweden, travelling together on a tour of Europe. There would also be Lynne from Bristol, who hadn't arrived yet.

"Lynne has called and ees on next train," Adela announced as she brought in the steaming tortellini.

Tony, the tutor, had retired to his room to prepare the following morning's class, so they finished the evening with light chat and drinks, lounging on the sofas in front of the open patio doors, enjoying the cooling evening air that drifted in from the garden. Shortly after everyone had retired, and Adela was about to leave for her home in the village, Lynne arrived.

"Soreee, I got a bit lost."

Her shrill voice echoed round the hall, disturbing the silence of the house, and Ben stirred in his sleep, nudged from his dreams.

***

"So, it looks like we are all hoping to get something different from this week's course."

Tony, the tutor, remarked as he handed around sketch pads and sets of pastels the following morning. Denim clad and balding, Tony had the air of a genial tour guide as he explained.

"I know some of you are new to painting and drawing but don't feel under pressure – just do what you can, experiment and enjoy yourselves. I've lived in Spain for several years now, running courses for Creativz Holidays, and the whole point of these breaks is you have fun and hopefully go home inspired. This morning we are going to spend a couple of hours looking at light and shade, how shadows are actually composed of colour and not just a flat grey or black, as most people assume. I think we'll start in the back courtyard with the fig tree there as it offers a great subject. We'll stop about midday for lunch and free time."

The group settled themselves on fold out chairs, eager to start, and Ben now noticed the shrill woman who'd arrived last night. She'd set herself on the edge of the group, her face half hidden under a large straw sun-hat. He guessed her age as around thirty-ish. Her frothy cream sun dress and carefully waved blonde hair gave her the air of a model for a herbal shampoo advert. She'd barely spoken at breakfast, except to introduce herself as 'Lynne with an e,' but everyone had welcomed her politely. The group had already bonded over the evening meal and drinks, and now Lynne offered a ruffle of newness and curiosity again.

The first session over, everyone clustered around Tony to compare work and receive some feedback. As predicted, John had managed a slightly upmarket stick man version of the fig tree, while wife Iris had managed better. Tony assured her it was a good effort. The graphic designers had very different styles. Abby's rendition of the tree was executed in sharp lines and careful detail while Jo's was more abstract, bold splashes of pastel. Ben had made a fair effort and the two Swedish retirees laughed good naturedly at each others' attempts, displaying rainbow-stained fingers as evidence they'd got into the spirit of the workshop.

"Good." Tony grinned at the group. "This afternoon we'll try some pictures around the pool, looking at water and the shapes ripples make. And the good part is we can all have a swim afterwards before dinner tonight."

The group broke into whoops of approval and light hearted clapping. All except Lynne, who'd hung back.

"We'll break for lunch now, but we've not had a look at your work yet, Lynne. Do you want to share it with the group?"

The late arrival was standing apart, scowling from the shadows of the fig tree.

"No. No I don't!" Lynne snapped, her face dark with hostility.

Everyone turned to look at her.

"No one is going to take the mick, love," John offered kindly. "Look at my effort. I bet you can't have done worse than that."

"No, I really don't want to. Just leave me alone."

Lynne turned and fled into the garden, the straw hat falling from her head and bouncing on its green ribbon against her shoulders as she ran.

"I'll go after her," Tony said. "Please go for lunch. Adela's laid tables under the orange trees on the lawn."

Lynne's bizarre behaviour was the topic of conversation for a short time, until Tony returned with the sullen faced young woman. Grabbing some quiche and salad, she flounced away to sit on the garden wall, turning her back on the others.

All eyes turned to Tony, who shrugged as much as to say *I tried*.

"She is so rude," Iris snorted. "Why is she even here if she doesn't want to join in? What's her problem?"

***

Over the next three days the group relaxed and immersed themselves in the workshops. Everyone except Lynne, who seemed content to shun their company and keep herself apart. Her aloof manner quickly alienated them all, and Ben noted how even kindly Ingrid had given up trying to encourage her to join them. Lynne always sat at the back during the workshops, gripping her sketch pad to her lap, stony-faced and offering no comments in discussions. She had, however, taken a shine to Ben and grabbed at every opportunity to latch onto him. On the third morning, as they were about to start a sketching exercise in the sunny courtyard, Lynne sidled up to Ben.

"Ben, can you help me with this chair? I just can't unfold it – I'm so silly, I know."

Her slightly whiny voice scratched at his nerves as her fingers stroked his arm.

"Sure, no problem."

Ben, always helpful and polite, pulled the canvas seat out for her.

"Where do you want it?"

"Just here please."

She indicated a spot in the shade of the wall, away from the others but close to Ben's seat. During the session he was aware of her furtively studying him from under the brim of her sun-hat, and it made him feel uneasy, as though he were the field mouse being eyed up by the silent bird of prey soaring above.

By the end of the day, her flirting had began to wear thin on him, and her constant pawing at his arm and demanding his attention began to irritate him. At first it had been subtle remarks, such as did he think the pots were a good subject? But by the afternoon the whispered questions as she leant across to him were becoming more personal and intrusive. He was aware everyone else had noted he'd suddenly become the object of Lynne's attention too, and he found it embarrassing. It wasn't as though he were encouraging this odd woman's attention. He'd come here to lose himself in this painting experience and put aside the recent months of his life, if just for a short while.

When Tony suggested they take their easels down to the orchard, Lynne refused to go.

"I want to work on my own this afternoon. I think I'll get better work done."

"OK Lynne." Tony shrugged. "You're not obliged to do all the sessions. Feel free to drop out if you wish."

Ben, for one, was relieved as the group wandered off down to the orchard without her.

"Aren't you the favourite, eh?" Iris teased him as they settled their chairs and easels under the trees.

"I'd rather not be, if I'm honest," he replied quietly.

Come the evening, Lynne vanished to her room again with a plate of food, refusing to join the others around the dinner table. This surprised Ben after she'd shown such a craving for his company. Adela too had noticed her odd behaviour.

"That Lynne is strange," she commented as she brought in the paella and spotted the last guest missing once again. "I caught her dancing and posing in the hall in front of mirror this afternoon, dancing sort of sideways and swirling her skirts like leetle girls do when they are dressing up and posing. Very vain. She not all that to look at even. She 'as a horsey face and way too skinny."

"Yeah," Jo remarked. "She always makes her face up and dresses as though she believes she's going on some magazine photoshoot, not sitting in the countryside painting. It's like she doesn't have much of a grasp on reality."

"To be honest, I think she has some behavioural issues," Ingrid offered.

"Let's sneak a look at her sketch pad." Jo was on her feet. "She's left it on the hall table."

"I don't think we should."

Tony was obviously a little uncomfortable at this, but the others were keen to see what Lynne had been producing while they'd been down the orchard most of the day.

"Oh what!" Jo exclaimed, flicking through the pad.

Her expression was a mixture between astonishment and mockery as she offered the pages for the others to see. All of Lynne's sketches were of herself, portraits drawn in the mirror, other images set in fantasy settings. There was Lynne in her cream sundress, standing in her bedroom window, the lace on the dress coloured in with meticulous watercolour and pen detail. Then Lynne, at the same window in her straw hat, face half shadowed. There was even one of her naked, sprawled back on the bed, open-legged, and presumably drawn from the mirror on the wardrobe door in her room.

"Blimey, what's she on?" Iris remarked.

"See, vacuous and vain," Jo crowed.

"She has some artistic talent though," Tony mused. "The life drawings are well executed, if a little over-idealised versions of herself."

The sketch pad returned to the hall table, the group fell to discussing what to do on their day off in town tomorrow. None of the plans included Lynne.

***

As though she somehow knew she were the object of growing pity and dislike among the group, Lynne joined them on the trip into Gerona and seemed desperate to be a part of the day's exploring, even enthusiastic.

"Oh I really want to get to know everyone properly today," she gushed as they clambered aboard the hired mini-bus.

"Is she on some happy-juice medication?" Jo muttered sarcastically to Ben as she and Abby joined him in a row of seats. "She's left it a bit late to become everyone's buddy all of a sudden."

"Maybe we should give her a chance," Ben responded. "She probably realises she's started off on the wrong foot and is trying to compensate now."

He noted with relief Lynne was forced to sit at the back away from him, but he also noted the dagger glare she gave Jo as she arranged herself next to the Swedish retirees.

Unfortunately for Lynne, her shrill chatter about her personal life, past boyfriends and favourite fashion designers quickly bored and exasperated the others during the drive. The group had planned on just having a quiet day exploring the old medieval part of the town and relaxing over a light cafe lunch, but Lynne managed to intrude into that, insisting it was all boring and the clothes shops were the only things worth seeing. In high glittery sandals, she staggered painfully over the cobbled streets, forcing the others to frequently wait for her as she hopped behind, complaining about blisters. Her braying giggle "oh, soreee don't wait for me" soon wore thin on them, and by the time the mini-bus came to pick them up in the square they were exhausted with her.

"Quick, sit next to us." Jo motioned to Ben, who was glad to oblige.

Lynne shot them a searing look and Jo glared stonily back.

"There's a seat here, Lynne," Ingrid offered kindly.

Back at the house, the group settled for the evening meal. Surprisingly, Lynne joined them. But, as she'd done during the trip, she launched into one of her self-absorbed tales in her nasal voice, interrupting and talking over the others.

"Then there was Charles. He was besotted with me and he looked a bit like you, Ben, dark and handsome. How old are you, Ben? You might be younger than him actually. The girls at work were so jealous of me."

Lynne's shrill, whinnying laugh cut across the table like a glass shard. The vegetable bowl passed hand to hand in tense silence.

"Yes, you've told us all this already, Lynne. Can we change the subject now?" Ingrid commented tersely. "Ben, you said your wife taught here for a while?"

"Yeah, Sue worked for Creativz as a summer break tutor for a few years before we met, doing what Tony does...here, in fact, at this house."

"She didn't want to come with you?" Iris asked.

Ben took a moment to answer.

"She died last August from stomach cancer. We'd arranged to come here together and I'd hoped she would live long enough to make it. It would have been her thirty fourth birthday tomorrow. She made me promise to come without her if......"

His voice choked off and the group fell into an awkward silence.

Ingrid got to her feet and walked around the table to enfold Ben in a motherly hug.

"I'm so sorry dear. This must be so hard for you. I expect Sue is with you in spirit though."

Suddenly Lynne broke out in a shriek.

"Ghostly Sue, here in spirit. Whooo. Are you with us now, Sue?"

"Oh shut up you stupid, insensitive woman!" It was Iris who turned venomously on her. "What a thing to say."

Lynne leapt to her feet, eyes spilling tears.

"Why are you all so against me? It's just because I was the last to arrive, isn't it. You've all ganged up on me because of that. You're all so nasty!"

Jo returned the volley, unable to contain her fury.

"No, it's because you are fucking irritating, selfish and ill mannered, and you're wrecking the holiday for everyone here with your pathetic, attention-seeking behaviour!"

Lynne glared around at the company and flounced out of the room. They could hear her sobbing loudly in the hall. No one rose to check on her. Jo scowled at her plate while the others sat dumbfounded, the veneer of table-talk politeness now shattered. Ben was clutching his fork so tightly that his knuckles turned as white as the bones beneath them.

"Are you OK Ben?" Ingrid asked quietly.

"Yeah, fine. I'll let it go over my head. I think you're right. Maybe she has mental problems and doesn't see how her behaviour is inappropriate. We need to be understanding."

"Does she genuinely have a personality disorder, or maybe she's just a nasty, selfish piece of work?" John added.

After dinner, Ben sat for a while on his balcony, watching the sun paint the evening sky purple as it sank behind the cypress trees. The faint tinkle of the fountain carried on the sultry air. As the full moon rose, a pearl dish in the sky, he fell asleep in the chair and dreamed of Sue, the Sue before cancer had ravaged her. She was wandering the dark gardens with him, enjoying the night perfume of the plants, their hands entwined. Then he was rudely jolted awake, the dream ruined, by urgent tapping at the door.

"Ben, can I come in and sleep with you tonight?"

It was Lynne, pleading.

"Why?"

Ben was immediately on his guard.

"I'm scared. I think there are ghosts here."

"There's no ghosts. Please go to bed, Lynne."

"Ben, please. I'm soreee. Just let me in."

The insistent knocking at the door continued and the handle started to rattle as Lynne tried to force her way in, but he'd bolted the door.

"Ben, can I come in? I can do dirty stuff if you want it."

Exasperated, Ben rose and shouted against the wood of the door.

"Go to bed, for Godsake! I'm not interested in you. I don't want anything from you. Just leave me alone."

He could make out Lynne muttering something menacingly against the other side of the door, then heard her feet skittering away down the corridor. Relieved, he climbed under the duvet and lay there, trying to calm his frayed nerves. This trip had been fraught enough due to its significance, and he really didn't need to be the focus of some deranged woman's obsession.

***

Everyone said their goodbyes to Tony on the Friday afternoon and spent the rest of the day amusing themselves now the break was officially over. Adela left them a cold supper and promised to be back to see them off in the morning.

Jo, Abby, Helgi and Ingrid took to the pool while Ben commandeered a sun lounger on the side with a book. Iris and John had taken a stroll to the village for the last time and Lynne, thankfully everyone agreed, was nowhere to be seen.

The late afternoon heat lay like a blanket across the countryside, stunning even the chirruping insects into silence, and water splashes from the laughing swimmers dried almost as soon as they hit the mosaic tiles surrounding the pool.

"Victory for the oldie." Ingrid laughed, touching the poolside as the other women floundered up behind her. "Last race and I've won three out of five."

"You do have the advantage of being a former athletics champion, dear," her friend Helgi reminded her.

The sun was starting to drop into the cypress trees as they finally clambered out, grabbing up towels.

"I'll bring some wine out for you energetic ladies," Ben offered.

As he returned with glasses and a bottle of sparkling white on a tray, Lynne appeared around the side of the house, swaying and staggering from side to side on her glittery heels.

"Aw is that for me, Ben. How kind," she slurred.

There was something unpleasant in her manner, in the twisted sneer across her face. Ben answered warily.

"You're welcome to a glass, Lynne. Here take this seat."

"Aww, sweet," she mocked, staggering towards the wicker chair he'd pulled out. Everyone noticeably stiffened and the light-hearted banter immediately ceased in anticipation of some scene erupting. But Lynne's manner suddenly changed and she lunged playfully at Ben, giggling as she grabbed him.

"Get off me, please Lynne."

He tried to gently dislodge her, but she clung on and tried to kiss him, arms drunkenly hooked around his shoulders.

"You can kiss me, Ben. Go on. I know you'd like to finger my pussy."

Grabbing his hand, she attempted to force it under her dress.

"Let go of me, Lynne."

Ben's desperate shove sent her staggering backwards to fall, arms flailing wildly, into the pool. Jo shrieked with delight and the others rose anxiously, all expecting to see an angry Lynne burst, spluttering, from the turquoise water. But she didn't resurface. She remained a rippling pattern of flowery dress under the water, and it eventually dawned on the watchers she was on the bottom of the pool and not moving. It was Ben that broke the moment and dived in, pulling her up and to the poolside.

"Here, can someone help me? I don't think she's breathing."

The others helped haul Lynn onto the tiles and Ingrid, calm and first aid trained, took control, checking for signs of breathing and a pulse. As Ingrid attempted first mouth to mouth and then full CPR, Ben groaned.

"Oh God, this can't be happening."

Ingrid worked for nearly ten minutes while Ben attempted to call an ambulance on his mobile.

"I can't get a local inquiry number. My phone isn't set up for Spanish networks," he burst out, panic rising.

Ingrid finally looked up from the stricken Lynne and announced flatly to the horrified onlookers.

"She's dead."

"Oh God. I didn't mean to hurt her, just get her off me."

Ben sat down abruptly on a lounger, white-faced and shaking. "I really didn't mean to push her in. I didn't even push her hard."

The large bruise and egg sized lump now appearing on Lynne's forehead told them she'd likely hit her head on the bottom of the pool.

"I killed her. I didn't mean it, I really didn't." Ben's voice was creeping towards hysteria.

"She was drunk and stumbled. You're not to blame, Ben," Ingrid said calmly. "We need to alert the authorities. Let's get her up onto a lounger."

Lynne was laid out on a plastic sun lounger and the group gathered around, shocked and silent. Ingrid tried the house phone, but the Spanish operator spoke no English and she gave up in frustration.

"I'll be charged with murder." Ben sobbed as he looked desperately around at the others.

"Ben," Ingrid reasoned. "We all saw what happened. We're witnesses. It was an unfortunate accident."

Everyone murmured agreement.

"What if the police don't believe that?" Ben whispered.

"Maybe we should call Adela or Tony. They can translate for the police and tell them what happened."

Then they realised no one had a contact number for either of them, and the Creativz office in London was closed at that time in the evening. So they agreed it was best to leave Lynne where she was until morning, as the poolside would no doubt be considered a crime scene anyway. When Adela arrived she could help them explain to the police. It was now getting dark and the group huddled around on the lounge sofas, saying little but finding comfort in each other's company and a bottle of brandy. No one felt like eating the supper, but all seemed reluctant to go to bed.

"Someone should cover her up," Jo murmured after a while, pulling a throw from one of the chairs. "I wish I hadn't been so mean to her now, saying those things."

She went outside with Iris. The dark garden hummed with night insects and the perfume of scented stock. Lynne, pale and still, looked almost regal under the moonlight, as though made of alabaster. The large bruise on her forehead glared vivid purple, as though someone had daubed her absent-mindedly with paint.

"Adela will know what to do," Jo whispered tearfully. "Poor Lynne."

***

Ben looked pale and drawn the following morning, having slept little. Everyone had drifted down to the dining room to await Adela, who arrived in sprightly form on her push bike just after seven.

"So, who wants cooked breakfast before we go our ways?" She beamed around at everyone, then quickly dropped the smile, eyeing them curiously. "What's wrong?"

"You didn't see Lynne outside on the lounger?" Iris asked.

Everyone broke into a panicky babble of explanation at once. After Lynne's body had been loaded into an ambulance, the police officer in charge spoke to Adela for some time. She explained to the anxious holiday-makers.

"Oh, poor Lynne. I told them it was all a horrible accident. They will inform the British police to tell 'er parents. The detective will want to interview everyone. They will organise a translator this afternoon so I'm afraid you all 'ave to stay until they've taken statements."

***

Ben dozed on the train as it sped across the Spanish countryside. Never had he been more grateful to slump into a carriage seat, clutching a ticket bound for England. The Spanish police had taken statements and contact details from everyone at the farmhouse. Ben hadn't been charged with any offence, although he had been warned he could be recalled for further questioning following forensic reports.

Two train changes later, he stepped off at London's Kings Cross, then caught a taxi to his modest flat in Putney. It was a bachelor pad he'd bought after selling the house following Sue's death. To continue to live in the home they'd chosen together, or sleep anymore in the bedroom they'd shared together, had become unbearable.

Ben gratefully dropped his rucksack on the hall floor. The bedroom spotlights softly obscured the view of the Thames and Putney Bridge beyond as he slipped down the blind. He slept deeply, emotionally exhausted from the past few days. His dreams were again of Sue, her sleeping face turned to him as she lay beside him. In the dream, he watched her until her eyes fluttered awake like hummingbirds wings, as vibrant and sparkling as the bird itself and as lovely. The dawn light through the blinds painted stripes on them as they slowly made love, daubing their bare skin with a slatted pattern of honey and copper.

He awoke abruptly with a gasp as Sue's face morphed into Lynne's, and that woman's hee-hawing, manic laugh drowned out Sue's gentle murmur in his mind. Throwing the bedclothes aside, Ben headed for the kitchen, suddenly hungry. The kitchen clock ticked nearly three in the morning.

There was little in the fridge as he'd cleared it out before the trip to Spain, but he remembered there were some crumpets in the freezer. Munching toasted crumpets at the kitchen table, Ben started to feel uneasy, as though someone else were in his apartment and watching him. Telling himself it was just his imagination due to stress, he headed back to the bedroom. No sooner had he fallen back into bed when he heard a distinct tapping on the bedroom door, like knuckles hitting wood. He started upright in the dark, listening keenly, but the sound suddenly stopped.

Drifting back to sleep, he was startled awake again by the insistent knocking, which sounded louder and more urgent now. Alarmed, he switched on the lamp, every nerve jangling. His first thought was someone had broken in, but then came a distinct murmur from just outside the bedroom door.

"I'm soreeee. Please let me in, Ben."

The tone was taunting, sly and mocking.

Horrified, he was out of bed and wrenching open the door. As he stood staring into the darkness of the hallway, his prickling senses told him he was being furtively studied by someone lurking just at the end of the hall. He was sure he caught a glimpse of a shadowy figure, slipping past the moonlit hall mirror, although it was little more than a brief movement. The silence was stifling as he stood, frozen, watching. Again, he saw a vague female outline near the front door, and then a flash of scampering, glittery high heels, darting away into the kitchen. Shaking, Ben switched on all the lights as he made his way through the flat, thoroughly checking every room, but he quickly realised no one was there with him. But he was certain he'd heard *her* voice, with its nasal, whiny edge.

No sooner had he climbed back into bed when the tapping starting again at the bedroom door. That unmistakable voice came again, whispering through the wood.

"I'm soreee. Can I come in, Ben? I can do dirty things if you want."

"Oh God! Please just leave me alone!" Ben yelled desperately into the darkness.

A cold sweat dampened his shirt and he realised he was trembling all over. There was a spiteful giggle and then silence fell again. Ben stayed awake the rest of the night with the lamp blazing, his nerves shredded.

Still shaken, trying to convince himself that the night's events had been down to an over-active imagination and stress, he went for a shower as dawn touched the river outside the windows. Before he reached the bathroom door across the hall, however, something sent his heart leaping to hammer at his ribs.

"No!"

The wet handprints along the wallpaper of the hall stood out starkly, following the trail of drips on the lino tiles. Drips that filled the gaps between the wet footprints of a heeled ladies shoe.

The Chrysalis

It hung between two dried-up daisy stems at the bottom of the garden, an oddly shaped little chrysalis catching the last rays of the weak October sun. Its silky webbing case shimmered in the sunlight, and Jude peered closer, fascinated. It appeared to be woven around a winged sycamore seed, this two inch pod of gossamer perfection, as she could make out the skeletal wings of the seed through the web. She wondered what was inside. Careful not to disturb or damage it as she tidied the flower bed, Jude moved on.

New to gardening and new to this house, with its huge rambling garden that backed onto the woods, she didn't want to mess up any eco-system with her clumsiness and lack of knowledge. That wouldn't do and her friend Joe, the saint of all things recyclable, re-workable and re-claimable, would probably make some cutting comment if she did. She'd begun to despair of ever getting his house rules right, and had mostly failed to remember how his composting system worked. She was aware that her six year old daughter, Emma, had developed a certain wariness of Joe too since they'd moved in here.

"Mum, why does he tell me off for putting teabags in the bin in the kitchen?" She'd asked, soon after their arrival.

"Er, I think they're supposed to go in the green bin outside the back door," Jude had sighed.

Perhaps she and Emma shouldn't have moved in here after all. It had been a step in desperation, if she were honest. Her lease had expired and the landlord had put their home up for sale.

"Why don't you move in with me for a while, just until you get sorted," Joe, a sandy-haired, bearded figure with something of the garden gnome about him, had suggested. It had seemed a good idea at the time, and a kind offer from her friend on the Neighbourhood Committee. But she'd come to realise that bachelor Joe, always full of sensible suggestions about bus lanes, community allotments and so forth at meetings, was just a little obsessive, even controlling, at home.

To make some compensation for the rent-free rooms she and Emma had taken at the top of Joe's house, Jude tried to help around the place while her daughter was at school and Joe was at work. Today she'd decided to tidy the garden. She'd picked up two binfuls of crisping autumn leaves already, keeping some back for Emma to make pictures with. She recognised oak and horse chestnut leaves among those blown over from the woods beyond, but couldn't name any of the others.

The little chrysalis caught her eye again as she returned the bin to the shed. It glistened as it moved in the breeze that stirred the seed heads, turning slowly on its silk ropes like a circus performer. Peering at it again, Jude could now make out eyes.

Yes she was sure there were two large dark eyes gazing back from behind the silk wall and she was sure they'd just blinked at her. She busied herself for another hour then, curiosity stirred, she went to look at it again. Whatever it was, waiting in there for the moment that Mother Nature called it forth, had closed its eyes now. But the pod looked fatter, fuller. 'In just that short time,' she wondered, 'so much has changed.' When the resident squirmed, she gasped and stepped back. For all her fascination, she wasn't a fan of insects and the thought this may pop open and disgorge the whatever-was-inside to fly into her hair now alarmed her a little. Jude decided to call it a day and go indoors to start dinner.

***

For the next three mornings Jude checked on the chrysalis, her curiosity getting the better of her. On the third day it was spangled with a light frost and she thought 'surely the cold will kill it?' As if it understood her concern, the big dark eyes opened again to peer at her through the thin gossamer web and she wondered again what sort of moth or butterfly was tucked inside. They considered each other for a moment, she and the whatever-bug, before the eyes closed once more and the little bundle shivered.

That evening over supper she asked Joe what moths or butterflies would be hibernating in the garden at this time of year? He replied that he was pretty sure none would be, but Jude wanted to know what it was and for Joe, the gardening expert, to see it.

"Let's go down to look then," he agreed, rising from the table.

Jude led the way with the torch, the beam chasing dancing monster-shapes behind the shrubs as they walked the path to the bottom of the garden. But when they reached the chrysalis it was just an empty, shredded piece of silk.

"Well, whatever it was has gone now," Joe stated the obvious.

Jude felt just a tiny bit disappointed. She would have liked to have seen the insect emerge, be able to identify it in one of Joe's wildlife books, to have felt knowledgeable for once and not the dummy when it came to all things environmental and green. Now it would remain just an unsolved mystery. They trudged back to the house in silence, as the wind stirred the branches of the trees in the wood beyond the fence.

***

Emma woke her at 2am, tugging her arm and whispering.

"Mum, come and see the tiny man in my room."

Jude was concerned that Emma would disturb Joe on the floor below, and he'd already complained that she was too noisy around the house. Creeping to her daughter's room, she wondered what had prompted this night time fantasy. Her eyes adjusted to the glow of the Barbie nightlite, and Emma pointed triumphantly at the chest of drawers by the window.

Jude was amazed to see there was indeed a tiny, naked man, about a foot high, perched on the chest and illuminated by a soft, blue glow. He appeared damp, his long silver-white hair plastered to his face and shoulders, as though he'd been caught in the rain. Or perhaps had recently been born. Moving closer, Jude was fascinated to see he sported a pair of incredible silvery green wings, which he'd unfurled and was apparently in the process of trying to dry and straighten out. He peered back at her with the dark eyes that she was sure had regarded her from the chrysalis, and threads of torn silk still clung to the long insect-like proboscis that served as a nose.

They regarded each other for a moment, then the tiny form took a leap into the air and flapped its wings. Jude leapt back with a loud cry, knocking over a stool. The creature seemed to quickly master its new wings and flew out of the open bedroom door and into the bathroom opposite. She and Emma ran after it and were just in time to see a blue globe of light exit the bathroom window, which Jude had left open.

"Mum, was it a fairy?" Emma cried excitedly, forgetting the silence after 9pm house rule.

"Shh, I don't know. Wasn't that amazing though?"

At that moment Joe yelled up the stairs.

"What's going on up there?"

"Er, nothing, Joe. Emma just had a bad dream."

She heard him stomp back into his study and slam the door, and she could almost feel his prickling irritation on the atmosphere.

"Do you think it will come back?" Emma whispered as they returned to her room.

"I don't know, darling."

Jude studied the damp marks on the top of the chest, noting the tiny footprints where the creature had stood. Then she turned to tuck her daughter back into bed, still in awe and disbelief at what she'd just seen. Surely such things didn't, couldn't, exist here, or anywhere come to think of it? But they'd both seen the tiny man with wings and there was no explanation for it.

***

Joe seemed to withdraw into himself over the next couple of weeks. He had never been a very sociable man, although he was highly respected on the Neighbourhood Committee. Jude had to admit she didn't really know much about his past life, only the snippets he'd given away over shared suppers when she and Emma had first moved in. She knew he'd once worked for the Royal Horticultural Society and was now employed by a local college as a part-time lecturer and researcher on organic self-sufficiency. His main love was gardening and, even at this time of year, the abundant greenhouse spilled with exotic fruit, many varieties of chilli peppers and herbs. But Joe tended to keep pretty much to himself of an evening, shut away in his study, leaving Emma and herself to make their own entertainment upstairs. She had the impression that he was not a happy man, deep down, and was looking for something else, something profound, to shape his life. He'd hinted as much one morning, while making a sandwich to take to work.

"Don't you ever wish there was more to life than this dull, earthly existence, Jude?" He'd remarked, out of the blue. "Something inspiring, other-worldly. I envy the plants in the garden their existence sometimes. They don't have to think, or worry and make decisions, they just follow their genetic blueprint, grow, produce seed and flowers, fulfilling each yearly cycle. How lovely to have nothing else to concern yourself with but to just exist and 'be.' What a joy and a freedom that must be."

Jude had been putting Emma's school bag together at the time. She'd turned to glance at him, surprised. Joe was not a man for emotional expression in general. She'd not known how to respond to this sudden outpouring, so she'd just shrugged and mumbled.

"I suppose so. Emma often says she'd like to be a bird or butterfly in the garden, not a care in the world, just being pretty."

"Yes, not a care in the world. What a lovely thought."

A pale, sad expression had crossed Joe's face momentarily, before he'd busied himself again, putting cheese and margarine back in the fridge.

Taking a sneaky look around the house when they'd first moved in, Jude had spotted many books on folklore and earth magic, leylines, astrology and suchlike, on the bookshelves in the study, alongside more conventional topics of eco-culture and green living. She would have liked to have taken a good look at some of the books, but Joe had started locking that room now and had become quite secretive about his research and personal interests.

At dinner he did sometimes talk briskly about eco-politics, permaculture and climate change, and Jude felt left behind and stupid. She felt these were topics she *should* care about and take an interest in, but somehow all the noise of daily living and Emma just left no time for quietly sitting down with a book anymore.

So she decided to make time and, that evening, instead of switching on the TV after Emma had gone to bed, she went down to the study to ask Joe if he would recommend a good book to get her started on organic gardening. She'd heard him go in there earlier after he'd bid her a polite good evening. Lamplight spilled over her toes from under the badly fitting door, and Jude was about to raise her knuckles to tap on the door, when she heard Joe exclaim.

"And those are your terms? Yes, I understand that once I've signed up to the process there's no going back."

A pause as though he were listening to a reply. Then Joe again.

"On Friday night then. I'll be ready. Thank you. No, I'm sure I won't regret it."

There was a nervous edge to his voice, but also what sounded like excitement too. Feeling like a nosy neighbour, Jude crept away down the hall where she spotted Joe's mobile on the hall table. There was no landline in the house, so who had he been talking to in the study, she wondered?

***

On the Saturday, having dropped Emma at her friend's, Jude returned to the house. Joe had told them that he would be working from home over the weekend, finishing a paper for the college, so she'd thought it wise to arrange for Emma to stay away overnight, just to ensure she didn't disturb him. Yet more conflict over Emma running up the stairs, singing in her room or using the wrong tea towel when drying dishes, she could not take.

Joe had seemed more intense and withdrawn the past few days, and often left his house guests to eat alone of an evening. She felt she should try and reach out to this obviously troubled man after all he'd done to help her and her daughter, but somehow she couldn't find a way, or the words to start a conversation. Yesterday she'd signed the lease for a small flat on the other side of town. It would mean a longer journey to school each day, but Jude had decided it was probably best if they gave Joe his space back and moved out. She planned telling him over supper that evening, thanking him of course for his hospitality and kindness in temporarily putting them up, but politely explaining they didn't want to be a burden any more.

The morning's frost still iced the gutters and hedges, but it was something more than the winter chill that made her shudder as she hung up her coat on the hall stand. She'd expected to return to find Joe in his study or front room, bent over his laptop with the log fire blazing. He'd not been up when she and Emma had left, but it was past ten in the morning now, and the house was silent and cold. She knew enough about her friend's habits to think this was odd, Joe being an early-bird, and one of the first things he did of a morning was to stir up the fire in the front room.

She checked the kitchen, the study, then tapped politely on his bedroom door to offer a cup of tea, but he was not home. 'Oh well', Jude thought. 'Maybe he's decided to go to the college to work after all.'

That was when she spotted the muddy footprints all over the tiled floor in the kitchen. Tiny, naked footprints, smaller than a toddler's, scattered around as though one or more small people had been running hither and thither. She was sure they'd not been there when she and Emma had left. Bending closer to examine them, she realised the prints actually looked very odd, almost human yet not. The toes were long and the feet seemed to have just three on each foot, plus the instep was very deeply inset. She remembered the damp prints the fairy man had made on the chest in Emma's room, and thought they looked similar. Uneasy at that thought, Jude went to the back door to check it. It had been unlocked, she presumed by her friend, which suggested he was in the greenhouse or shed, so she went outside to call him and ask him to come and look at the odd prints.

But Joe was nowhere to be found. Jude walked to the end of the garden, tucking her hands inside her jumper sleeves to try and warm them, her breath misting on the air. As she turned back to the house, she spotted the chrysalis hanging between two branches of the cherry tree, and she let out a little shriek. The silken cocoon was the size and vaguely the shape of a human being, and the white webbing glistened with frost. It must have been there all night. But what on earth had made such a thing and, more importantly, what was inside it? Gathering her courage, Jude crept up to it. She spotted something snagged among the threads. It was a large silver ring with a red stone, which she recognised immediately as Joe's.

"Oh God!"

Jude stumbled backwards and fled to the house. Back inside, she was sure she could hear scuttling and whispering upstairs, and realised that the makers of the muddy footprints in the kitchen must be up there. Steeling her nerves, she crept quietly up the hall and, sure enough, the footprints carried on up the stairs, boldly marking the polished oak treads. Debating whether to go up or not, her nerves finally failed her and she retreated, frightened, back to the kitchen. But now she realised she was vulnerable should the print-makers come back downstairs to leave the way they'd presumably come, through the back door. She could see the door of Joe's study from here and it was surprisingly open, so she shut herself inside, taking the large brass key that had been left in the lock to lock it from the inside. Breathing heavily, she pushed the bulky leather reading chair against the door for good measure.

Struggling to calm herself and get a grip, she realised she'd left her phone in her bag on the hall table. But if she called the police, what would she say? My friend has disappeared and there's a huge chrysalis that could contain him, hanging in the garden? From the study she had a good view of the garden and that dreadful gossamer pod hanging motionless in the cherry tree.

It was some time before she heard the intruders scamper past the door, tiny bare footsteps slapping on the tiles as they headed for the kitchen. The door out to the garden slammed and she heard whispered chattering pass by underneath the study window, small voices, almost like a breeze sighing. Peering out, she could see nothing, only the bamboo stems in the bed directly to the left stirring, as though something small was pushing its way through them.

Movement in the cherry tree caught her eye and, to her horror and amazement, the chrysalis began to struggle, squirming as though something were trying to break free. Her view was partly obscured by the dense branches but she thought she saw something emerge, something large, white, naked, that scrambled onto a branch above, teetering there for a moment or two, before it swept up into the sky, its large, silvery wings sending the last leaves of the cherry tree showering to the ground in a golden curtain as it took off. She watched the being swoop to the end of the garden, to glide silently over the fence and into the dark forest beyond.

By the time Jude had gathered her wits enough to leave the study and start packing hers and Emma's suitcase, dusk had begun to creep up the garden from the dense woods around the house. Way off in the trees, the first owls began to call. One cry, a high, peeping wail, ended uncannily in a rattle of almost human laughter. It was a sound that perhaps celebrated freedom and the joy of simply being alive.

Bloody Christmas

That's what Mum always called it anyway, Bloody Christmas. It was so much hassle, she said, and where do we find money for presents, fancy food, blah blah, kids always want everything they see on the bloody telly. In truth, Ben, my six year old brother, and I didn't and were quite happy with what we were given. But Christmas of '93 really was a terrible one.

It had started with Mum losing it on Christmas Eve when she and Dad had a blazing row and she chucked the frozen turkey at him. He'd ventured into the hellhole that was the kitchen, lair of stressed-out Mum trying to follow Delia recipes for stuffing and trimmings. I guess Dad had thought he was being helpful instead of interfering. Anyway, he was floored by the turkey, smashing his head into the door frame and knocking himself out as he fell.

"Oh God. No. He's dead!"

Mum, as always over the top, scrambled for a tea towel to stem the ribbon of blood creeping across the lino from Dad's head.

"Dan, don't stand there like a lemon! Call an ambulance."

I did. Dad wasn't dead but he was badly concussed and had a fractured skull, we found out later. Of course Mum had to stay at the hospital as she was convinced he was at death's door so Ben and I were dragged along to sit in the hospital waiting room. Mum had called Granny Brent to pick us up. She came sweeping into the room in a battered canvas coat that swirled around her calves, wellies, and long, wild white hair which gave her the appearance of a cross between a mad witch and Worzel Gummidge. Granny Brent was mum's mum and we didn't see her often, although she only lived a few miles out of town.

"Get in the car, boys. Mind you sit on the plastic and don't touch the gun," she said.

There was a shotgun across the back ledge of the rusty Volvo. Gran explained she'd been shooting rabbits 'for the pot' earlier, and hadn't expected to get a desperate call from Mum to keep us overnight.

"What's the smell, Gran?" I ventured as we sped off down the dual carriageway out of town.

"Ferrets," she replied bluntly. "In the back. They don't bite."

"Will we have Christmas turkey at your house tomorrow then?" Ben asked warily.

"I won't promise turkey, Ben, but I do have a lot of old chickens and we could maybe sacrifice one for Christmas Day."

Ben looked at me, his eyes wide with horror.

"Where did you think roast dinners came from, numpty?" I tormented him.

Gran turned the Volvo off the dual carriageway at the next roundabout and down a side road into dark countryside. We drove in silence for a long time, passing occasional pubs, their Christmas lights reflected onto wet car parks. Rudolph flashed idiotically on rooftops and blow up Santa's stomped across the fronts of the isolated, big houses dotted along the road. What fake bullshit, I thought. Everyone feels obliged to be jolly and get into the Christmas spirit. At thirteen, I was just entering that cynical age when the magical facade of childhood drops away and you start to see the world in a colder, harder light.

Streetlights finally vanished behind us and the car bumped around as Gran wrestled it along a dark, rutted track. Ben was fascinated as we drew into the yard. I vaguely knew the house but guessed Ben wouldn't remember it as he'd been really young when we'd last visited.

"Boys, go in and make yourselves at home."

The yard smelled of pigs and I could hear geese somewhere in the darkness nearby, cackling and hissing.

Gran let us into the house, and then went back outside to settle her ferrets in the shed for the night. We sat politely at the table, gazing around the old farmhouse kitchen.

"Wow. It's big. Granny lives here all on her own?" Ben asked.

"Yeah, Grandad died years ago but she still keeps lots of animals and sells stuff at the market, Mum says. There's fields at the back that go down to the woods. They had a Shetland pony once, called Lawnmower. You were still a baby then. I can only just remember him." I filled him in on the little I could recall.

Gran came back in, shrugging off her big coat.

"You boys must be hungry. I'll get some tea on."

Ben looked at me in desperation, eyes wide, whispering.

"Will she make me eat squirrels and rabbits?"

Gran caught our conversation and laughed.

"No, we're just having cheese on toast. Do you like cheese on toast, Ben?"

"Yes thanks." He looked relieved.

"Your mum promised to call before your bedtime to say goodnight and let us know how your dad is doing. I don't have a telly, only the radio I'm afraid, but there's lots of board games in the back room you can rummage through if you like."

Grans' brisk manner had softened a little and she smiled a lot, which made her look less witchy. We spent the next three hours playing Kerplunk, Buccaneer and Mousetrap together around the kitchen table, laughing and teasing each other when someone's plastic mouse ended up under the trap. Gran was really cool and let us stay up late, but I noticed she kept glancing out of the kitchen window when she got up to get us biscuits or juice, and then she locked the cat flap in the back door.

"Mind you don't go outside during the night. You boys promise me that? And don't unlock that cat flap, even if the cats are scratching at it to go out. They can use their litter tray indoors tonight."

When we went up to bed Ben was full of it and excited that Gran had said he could feed the chickens and check for eggs in the morning. I'd spoken briefly to Mum, who'd promised us a proper Christmas Day on Boxing Day instead when we could swap presents. I wasn't really bothered as the day was always full of Mum and Dad arguing anyway and some part of the dinner was usually burnt. We never went anywhere and no one came to visit us. Maybe the day at Gran's would be more fun. Mum had asked how we were getting on. She'd sounded a bit nervous. I'd replied we were fine and Gran was odd but in a nice way.

"I want to see all the animals tomorrow," Ben told me as he pulled off his jumper. "Gran says she's got some binoculars and we can go down in the woods and look for deer. Why didn't mum like living here?"

"I don't know. Why, what's she said?"

I was curious. He shrugged.

"Only that the house was scary so that's why Gran usually visits us and we don't get to come out here."

"Do you reckon it's scary here then?"

Ben pulled a thoughtful face.

"Nah. I like Gran. She's funny and doesn't nag on like Mum."

Gran left us in the big bedroom at the back, which had two single guest beds which she laid out with faded, worn sheets and pillowcases. It was all clean, she assured us, adding as she left.

"If you hear anything in the garden tonight it will be just foxes. So don't get concerned."

"Sure," I replied, puzzled why she should say such an odd thing.

As we'd been bundled off in such a hurry when the ambulance had arrived we had no pyjamas with us so went to bed in our pants and T-shirts. I was woken some time later by Ben, shaking me.

"Dan, quick! One of Santa's elves is in the garden."

"What? Don't be daft."

"It really is. There's a little man by the pond, eating the fish."

I reluctantly rose, wrapping the blanket round myself as the room was so cold. Snow was floating down outside and our breath misted the glass as we peered out of the window. As Ben said, there was a tiny human-like figure outside in the yard, squatting by the pond and gnawing on something, which looked more like one of the rabbits Gran had left to hang on the fence to me. The security light outside threw its shadow across the yard. It seemed to be wearing old brown trousers, jacket and a shapeless beanie hat, a bit like the pictures of medieval peasants in our school history books. Dark hair straggled out from underneath the cap and I guessed it must have been less than three feet tall.

"Maybe it's not an elf, Dan," Ben whispered. "Santa's elves are jolly and have red noses and green hats. What do you reckon it is?"

I replied I had no idea, and then the back door burst open below us and the flare and crack of Gran's shotgun lit up the yard as she fired into the air. The creature turned to fix her for a moment with black glittering eyes, and the face was like a shrivelled turnip, horrible and malevolent. It exposed tiny pointed teeth as it drew its lips back in a sneer. Then it was gone, dropping its meal from its gnarly fingers to scamper back down the garden, vanishing into the darkness beyond the hedge. Ben had cried out in fear as it had turned and we'd seen its face properly. I had to admit I was pretty creeped out too, my mind racing to work out what it was we'd just seen. A dressed-up pet monkey escaped from somewhere? Some sort of remote controlled puppet sent in as a joke by neighbours?

Gran came up the stairs to check on us.

"Are you boys OK? I hope the gun going off didn't scare you. I was just cleaning it and it went off by accident."

She obviously wasn't aware we'd been watching from the window. Ben had calmed down and surprised me by saying nothing. Maybe he was too upset and shocked. Gran tucked him in and left us again, this time with a nightlight which gave the faded room a warm glow. After a while Ben whispered to me.

"Will it come back do you think, Dan? Is that why Gran locked the cat flap, so it couldn't come in and get us, or eat the cats if they went outside in the night?"

"Maybe. We'll ask her in the morning."

He seemed content at that and went to sleep but I lay awake trying to figure it out. It must have been the early hours of Christmas Day when I heard something scrabbling in the bushes below our room. I got to the window just as the outside security light was triggered, flooding the yard below with cold yellow light. There it was again, the small goblin-thing padding across the yard, clutching the ripped up rabbit and gnawing on it as it scouted around on the ground. I guessed Gran must have been deeply asleep as she didn't rush out to confront it this time. It disappeared from view and I realised it must have gone under the lean-to porch to the back door.

A bit freaked out now but curious, I crept down the stairs to the kitchen and flicked on the light. The cats were in their basket but up on their feet, backs arched and hissing. Heart banging nervously, I went to the window and could see its shadow by the back door. I realised with a start it was scratching and probing at the cat flap. I went down on all fours so my face was level with the see-through little plastic door and I could make out its shape on the other side, muttering and gibbering. The sound made my blood run cold. It suddenly fell silent and pushed its face up against the clear plastic and I got a good look at its black, evil eyes peering menacingly through, right back at me. The shrivelled turnip face screwed up in the most horrible way as it bared its teeth and said something in that gibber. Then it scuttled away again. I went back to bed but didn't sleep well, worried it would come back and somehow find its way in.

Christmas Day dawned bright and fresh. Ben wasn't in his bed when I got up and not in the bathroom either. Gran wasn't up yet so I dressed and went downstairs, expecting to find Ben having breakfast in the kitchen. The back door was wide open.

Curious, I went out into the yard to call him, guessing he'd gone to check for eggs on his own as he waited for Gran to surface. Ben's trainer footprints were visible in the snow, walking out to the middle of the yard. I could also make out tiny boot prints running determinedly across the yard, something the size of a toddler, heading to meet him. Where they collided it looked like a scuffle had taken place and I followed the trail of drag and scuffle marks as they headed down the garden path, across the field, and towards the woods. By the wooden fence at the edge of the field the snow was churned with blood, and scraps of bloody orange cloth were snagged on the top rail, parts of Ben's favourite T-shirt that he'd worn to bed. I felt sick with concern now, terrified for my brother.

I realised I was shaking as I climbed the fence, intent on following the trail. It led me deeper into the woods where I began frantically calling him. Only the twittering of birds in the trees broke the silence. I stepped on something and stooped to look at it, jumping back when I realised it was a small beanie hat, just like the one the goblin-thing had been wearing. There was also a clump of ratty, straw-like dark hair in the snow. Ben had put up a fight, I thought. Good for him, but where was he now?

I ran back to the house to rouse Gran.

"A goblin took Ben," I shouted as I shook her awake. "He went outside last night. That thing you shot at has got him and dragged him into the woods."

Her face drained of all colour as she blinked at me.

"God, no! Dan, go back and keep looking while I get dressed. I'll be with you in a minute."

I did as she asked and ten minutes later she was beside me with her shotgun. We both stalked the woods, desperately calling Ben. The trail through the snow ended abruptly at a large mound in a clearing and Gran let out a horrified cry.

"It's taken him into the faery realm, the evil fey! Taken him into the Underworld."

"Why? What is a fey?" I asked, baffled.

Gran was close to tears and suddenly looked a hundred years old, her face haunted and withered.

"There are many creatures that share this world with us, Dan. Some good, some evil. That one has been visiting the farm for years, centuries for all I know, before your Grandfather and I ever owned the place. It always comes on Christmas Eve and I called it Jack Frost. So far it's only cost me the odd chicken over the years, but now this!"

"Maybe you should have shot it dead last night," I ventured.

"I don't know if they can be killed, Dan. But I wish I'd tried now."

The police arrived and made a thorough search of the wood. I overheard the crime scene officer telling Gran they'd found a chewed child's finger in the snow near the clearing. She started crying and I felt sick to my stomach again.

Ben was never found and Mum blamed Gran, furious with her. He was listed as another 'missing child,' suspected abducted by some pervert or weirdo. I've never had the courage to tell Mum about what I saw in the yard that night, but I suspect she may have had some idea of what had really happened. After all, she'd grown up in that house and she must have seen things over the years. That's why she was so scared to go back, even as a grown up.

Every Christmas Eve we light a candle for Ben and think of him. Mum cries. Dad usually gets drunk. Gran has sold the farm now and moved into an old people's maisonette in town, where she keeps to herself. I visit sometimes but we never speak of Ben.

About the Author

Steph has been a keen reader, writer and artist since childhood, brought up on a diet of graphic novels, ghost stories and sci-fi. Originally from the suburbs of London but now living in Bristol, UK, she spends her spare time writing. Her dark fiction stories range from tales set in dystopian futures, to dark literary fiction, ghost and classic horror stories. Some of these have been shortlisted in international writing competitions.

Her professional publishing history to date runs to several short stories, featured in horror anthologies produced by Horrified Press, Grinning Skull Press, Almond Press and Dark Alley Press, plus a novella by Dark Alley Press, *'The Tale of Storm Raven'*.

Steph also produces book cover illustrations, including the cover for this collection.

She has a website – **stephminns.weebly.com** – where you can read her stories, interviews and reviews.

She also has a Facebook fiction page - **https://www.facebook.com/stephminnsfiction**.

Printed in Great Britain
by Amazon